NEVERMORE

A TAMPA BAY TROPICS THRILLER

GEORGE L. FLEMING

ST. PETERSBURG PRESS

This is a work of fiction. Names, characters, businesses, places, events, locales, and incidents are either the products of the author's imagination or used in a fictitious manner. Any resemblance to actual persons, living or dead, or actual events is purely coincidental.

Published by St. Petersburg Press

St. Petersburg, FL

www.stpetersburgpress.com

Copyright ©2022

All rights reserved. No part of this publication may be reproduced, distributed, or transmitted in any form or by any means, including photocopying, recording or other electronic or mechanical methods, without the prior written permission of the publisher, except in the case of brief quotations embodied in critical reviews and certain other noncommercial uses permitted by copyright law. For permission requests contact St. Petersburg Press at www.stpetersburgpress.com.

Design and composition by St. Petersburg Press

Cover design by St. Petersburg Press and Isa Crosta

Paperback ISBN: 978-1-9403XX-XX-X

eBook ISBN: 978-1-9403XX-XX-X

First Edition

NEVERMORE

For Linda, the love of my life for forty-five years, the most patient and understanding person I have ever met, a woman whose intellect is matched only by her beauty, and, of course, the inspiration for Ms. Reed O'Hara.

I love you, my beautiful warrior. May our journey together never end.

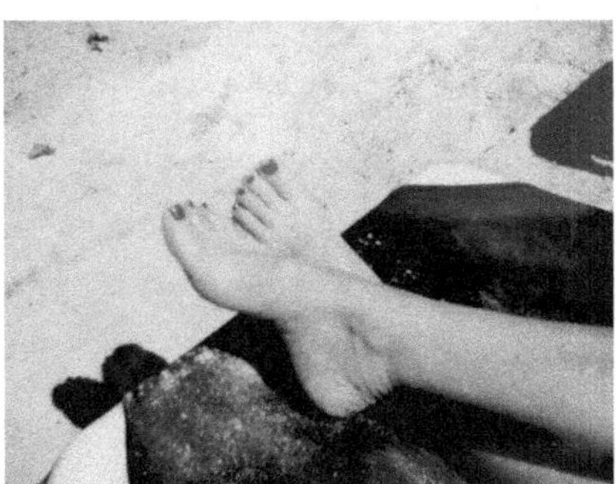

1

Christmas morning in Florida.

Just past eleven o'clock.

Tampa attorney Reed O'Hara was aglow from making love with her husband Jake Dupree on the king bed in their master bedroom.

Aided by a cloudless, Monet blue sky, the sun already had raised the temperature to a balmy eighty degrees. Reed decided to sunbathe in her new micro-bikini atop their penthouse terrace in downtown Tampa. Only modesty and the Florida Bar prevented her from doing away with her tan lines altogether by sunbathing nude.

Ever the prepared Girl Scout, Reed first applied SPF-30 sunscreen, then stretched out on a chaise lounge, keeping a bottle of Voss artesian water by her side. She figured she had thirty minutes to soak up the bright sunshine while Jake prepared a Christmas breakfast of scrambled eggs, fried potatoes with peppers and onions, medallions of beef tenderloin, and broiled Pomodoro di Pachino tomatoes topped with blue cheese crumbles.

Within minutes, her lean, svelte body glistened with perspiration, though a light breeze, making wavelets across the nearby lap pool, kept her from getting over heated.

The breeze awakened the eight rose bushes lining both sides of the lap pool. The bushes were choked with Mr. Lincoln rose blooms, Jake's pride and joy. A rose aficionado, Jake considered Mr. Lincolns the most fragrant red roses in the world. He told anyone who would listen that the secret to growing healthy rose bushes was fortifying the soil with spent coffee grounds.

Though nearly ten feet away, Reed still picked up the alluring scent of the deep red velvet rose blooms.

Reed used an index finger to play idly with perspiration puddled in her navel.

She was reminded of how, as a child growing up in West Virginia, she couldn't resist jumping with both feet into rain puddles—wearing her bright red rubber rain boots, naturally.

Reed felt drowsy in the soothing tropical heat.

She drifted off to twenty years ago when she was a teenager in Charleston, West (By God) Virginia.

At thirteen, Reed was full of what the polite crowd called passion and persistence, but what her people, those of the hollers and cold creeks and coal mines, called piss and vinegar.

Even as a seventh grader at DuPont Junior High, she never hesitated to express an opinion or to defend herself inside or outside of the classroom.

Brilliant and hardworking, Reed saw herself as a kind of scholar athlete. She treated her academics and her sports as a gestalt, a unified whole.

She tore into nearly all of her classes: math, science, history, literature, geography. However, Spanish gave her fits because she couldn't bear to mispronounce a single Spanish word, and she disliked rolling her R's or pronouncing tildes. However, she regularly made straight A's, including Spanish, though she never again took up a foreign language after seventh grade.

And she happened to be a superb basketball player.

Only an inch over five-feet tall and weighing under ninety pounds, Reed made up for her lack of height and bulk with fierce quickness, deadly shooting accuracy, court savvy, and a total lack of fear.

Reed learned her craft by playing for hours and hours on a cracked cement outdoor court with plywood backboards and bent rims without nets. Every weekday afternoon, after finishing her homework, she and her dingy white Converse high-tops took off for the lone full court in her neighborhood of weathered Victorian homes, well-kept bungalows, and stoic trailers hoisted on cinder blocks and wrapped in white picket fences. Reed played basketball until the sun dropped behind the Blue Ridge Mountains.

On weekends, she got her Saturday chores done as quickly as possible, then spent the rest of the day on the basketball court.

But there never was any basketball on Sunday, which was reserved, without exception, for Bible class and service at Spring Fork Baptist Church in the morning, and then a sumptuous afternoon supper often including fried chicken, mashed potatoes topped with a crater of melted butter, green beans suffused with lard, and peach cobbler or coconut custard pie—sometimes both, even.

After evening service at Spring Fork Baptist, Reed came home and read stories by Mark Twain, Flannery O'Conner, and William Faulkner. Even when her parents banished her to bed, Reed hid under the covers and read with a flashlight. When she finally fell asleep, she dreamt of making the perfect pass, crashing the boards, or hitting the winning shot in the Yoknapatawhpha County basketball tournament.

An open-minded person who couldn't care less about a person's skin color or gender, Reed played basketball with boys and girls, some Black yet mostly white, and players of all ages --- tweens, teens, and those old enough to hop in a fast car and buy Bud Light at the Fas-Check Supermarket.

Her inclusiveness was a direct reaction to her father's extreme racism and ingrained sexism.

Sure enough, Reed became a court leader, directing teammates to move without the ball and to peel off toward the rim after setting a pick. She taught her teammates several plays, and woe be unto those who didn't run the play exactly as Reed designed it. Her no-look pass was a wonder to behold, and she showed impressive hops in her rebounding. Reed was fearless when driving to the basket and she never complained when she got bruised and battered under the rim.

"No blood, no foul" was her mantra.

However, just because she was tough didn't mean she was an idiot.

When Reed tried out for seventh grade basketball at DuPont Junior High School, she insisted on trying out for the boys' squad.

"Just being practical here, sir," Reed said to Gary Carter, DuPont's rotund principal.

"How so, young lady?" Principal Carter asked.

"There'll be too many stiffs on the girls' team, and playing with stiffs is how you blow a knee. Not being critical, just sensible."

"So you're not grandstanding here? Maybe looking for some attention by sporting for a fight?"

"No, sir. I only want to stay in one piece by playing with the best. I don't give a hoot about starting a dust up here."

Reed displayed her Mona Lisa smile, still in its prototype phase.

"I think I believe you, Miss O'Hara. But don't think I'm some hick from French Lick. I recognize that smile of yours. Italians call it 'sfumato'—you're being sly and equivocal."

Pleased with his observation, Principal Carter leaned far back in his executive chair, causing his substantial belly to rise like a Martian warship emerging ominously from beneath the ground, *War of the Worlds* style.

Reed leaned forward in her chair, her elbows resting on the chair arms, her hands folded.

"I'm sure I don't get your meaning, sir. But I appreciate your teaching me a new word—'sfumato', I like it."

However, Reed knew better than to underestimate her principal. She learned early on that he was a shrewd, educated, and kind man.

After all, in the first week of seventh grade at DuPont, Principal Carter singled out Reed and promptly introduced her to his fifty-volume set of the Harvard Classics that he kept in his office. He himself had read every book in the collection, twice.

With Principal Carter's guidance, Reed started with *The Meditations* by Marcus Aurelius, followed by Charles Darwin's *The Origin of Species*.

"Darwin isn't too popular in this neck of the woods, so I recommend you leave his book at home when you go to Bible class," Principal Carter told Reed.

"Good idea sir, I also like how the Harvard Classics was first marketed as 'Dr. Eliot's Five-Foot of Books', you know, because good things usually come in five-foot packages."

Principal Carter and Reed sat in silence for almost three minutes.

The only sound was the ticking of the schoolhouse regulator clock on the office wall—the principal could have gotten a silent clock, but he liked the ticking, since it reminded him not to waste a single minute of his life.

Finally, Principal Carter spoke.

"I'll tell you what, Coach says you're the best basketball player for your age in the Charleston area. So I'm going to let you try out for the boys' team—with you on the team, we might get a winning record."

"Thank you, thank you, sir. I won't let you down. I promise."

"See that you don't, Miss O'Hara, because I am going to get a lot of grief for doing this. Say a prayer for me this Sunday."

"Yes, sir. Glad to, really."

Principal Carter studied a report, signaling he was ready for this meeting to end.

"All right now, get on out of here before I change my ...."

He looked up from his paperwork: Reed was gone before he finished his sentence.

Faster than a chipmunk, just like Coach said, he thought.

After a successful tryout, Reed made the DuPont Panther's boys' seventh grade basketball team. During the first few practices, Reed displayed natural leadership skills by introducing herself with a firm handshake to each teammate; by gently criticizing or complementing a player in the course of running a play; by listening to Coach Wallace and putting into action his mandates; and by pouring over the team playbook at night with her flashlight and the bed sheet over her head.

Put succinctly, Reed led by example. Her teammates, though inclined to be sexist toward her, quickly saw it didn't matter a hill of pinto beans that she was a girl, resulting in Reed being the unanimous choice for team captain.

"Come on, Tommy, I said set a pick, not stand there and pick your nose," Reed said in a low voice during practice.

Tommy nodded sheepishly in agreement.

"Remember, T-Man, you're a DuPont Panther, always moving, always on the hunt, all right?"

Again, Tommy nodded in agreement, this time with more confidence.

He let out the best panther snarl he could muster.

The rest of the team, including Reed and Coach Wallace, joined Tommy in a group panther roar.

"Shoot, that girl already memorized the whole playbook," Tommy said while showering in the boys' locker room after practice.

"Heck, Tommy, I had the playbook memorized in only three days, it's called studying," Charley said as he soaped up his afro.

"Whatever, peckerwood, long as Reed keeps feeding me inside, I'll be a happy man."

Tommy's teammates hooted loudly, their laughter reverberating off the tiled shower walls.

"Better grow some more pubes before you call yourself a man, Tommy," Charley said.

More hoots. More laughter. Even Tommy joined in on the caterwauling.

Showering by herself in the girl's locker room, Reed heard the boys next door.

Good thing those knuckleheads can ball, she thought, as she rinsed out Prell shampoo from her long, golden blonde hair.

And ball the seventh-grade DuPont Panthers certainly did: in the first three games, the team won by an average margin of twenty-seven points.

After each of these three victories, Coach Wallace and the team gathered at center court and panther roared.

Principal Carter would stand off to the side, with his arms folded, smiling with pride.

Indeed, the season was looking up. That is, until it took a sharp turn south in the fourth game.

In the second half of that game, with DuPont holding a seventeen-point lead on its home court, Reed feigned a layup and dished the ball to Charley in the right corner. Charley caught Reed's pass and set up for a three-pointer. In a flash, an opposing player, who was white, charged into him. Falling backwards, Charley used his arms to cushion the fall. His right forearm snapped.

Charley's opponent stood over him and grinned.

"How you like that, Buckwheat," he growled with an ugly snarl.

Reed, who was standing next to the referee, heard the racial slur.

"Ref, did you hear what he just called Charley?"

The referee, who was white, shook his head no.

"Can't hear a thing with all those eight balls screaming in the stands."

With that, Reed picked up the basketball and threw it at the opposing player standing over Charley.

The basketball hit the boy in his face with Roman candle ferocity. Blood streamed out of his nose and into his mouth. He spit out the blood, spraying the court with a bright red mist. The boy put his right hand over his nose. Blood seeped between his fingers.

"You broke my nose, you midget!"

The boy charged at Reed.

Bad luck for him: Reed had been studying the Korean martial art tae kwon do for over a year in Charleston.

So she calmly side-kicked the boy in his stomach.

Reed dropped him like a bad habit.

The boy laid on the floor and curled into a fetal position.

But he recovered quickly and got up, wobbly, but standing nonetheless.

One tough country boy, Reed thought.

"Think you can go all kung phooey on me, little girl, I'm going to snap your neck like a chicken," the boy screamed.

Before Reed could react, Tommy jumped on the boy and pummeled him with his fists.

"That's my captain you're threatening, jerk face!"

And sure as Mountaineers rising early for Sunday service, a group brawl ensued.

Even Charley, broken arm and all, got into the melee by grabbing what he hoped was an opponent's leg and biting the ankle.

Coach Wallace got the better of the wrestling match between him and the other team's coach.

Principal Carter and two police officers finally restored order after ten minutes of dangerous chaos.

And the end result?

Coach Wallace was suspended for the remainder of the season. Fortunately, his wife Loretta, an algebra teacher at DuPont and former WVU power forward, stepped in to coach the boys' seventh-grade squad.

Reed was kicked off the team, as were Tommy and Charley.

Unsurprisingly, the seventh-grade Panthers did not win a single game for the rest of the season.

Principal Carter considered expelling Reed; instead, he gave her a five-day in-school suspension.

"I accept, Miss O'Hara, you were defending your teammate. After all, that racist troglodyte might have further injured Charley."

Reed didn't speak, only listened.

"However, you were team captain, the leader who sets the example for the team. It's a demanding role to play, and you still have a lot to learn, especially in understanding how your individual actions can have a rippling effect on those you lead."

Reed nodded yes.

"I believe with all my heart, Miss O'Hara, one day you will become a most excellent leader."

"Thank you, sir," Reed said stoically.

For five consecutive days, Reed sat in the principal's waiting room and read from the Harvard Classics, consuming the volumes of Homer's *The Odyssey* and *English Poetry I: Chaucer to Gray*.

If she came across a difficult passage, Principal Carter gladly explained it to her.

Reed especially enjoyed *Don Quixote* by Miguel de Cervantes. Though many readers saw Don Quixote as a chivalrous knight whose time had long past him, Reed thought he was a meddling old fool who should have known windmills were not dragons and that a peasant girl was not a damsel in distress.

Reed O'Hara was a clear-eyed realist even at thirteen.

And she had no idea how one day *Don Quixote* would figure so prominently in her adult life.

Though Reed never lost her love for basketball, she didn't play on another school team, as streetball was satisfying enough.

Besides, tae kwon do, where she could shatter pine boards and fight in tournaments to her heart's content, became a consuming passion in her life.

And what did Reed learn from that fateful fourth game of basketball at DuPont Junior High School?

"When I stand up for someone, I'm standing up for myself as well," Reed said as she came out of her dream state on the pool terrace of her downtown Tampa penthouse.

"What was that, my love?"

Jake stood by Reed's chaise lounge.

Reed slid her Wayfarer sunglasses down the bridge of her nose.

For a moment or two, she admired her tall, fit, and muscular husband.

"Oh nothing, Jake, I was just reminiscing."

"Well, breakfast is ready. Shall we eat inside?"

Reed rose from the lounge.

Jake held her in his arms.

The couple kissed passionately.

"Merry Christmas, my wild Irish rose."

"And Merry Christmas to you, my dear sweet husband."

They held hands as they walked across the terrace.

"Knock, knock," Jake said.

"Oh, no. All right. Who's there?"

"Aretha."

"Aretha who?"

"Aretha would look great above our fireplace right now."

Reed took off her sunglasses so Jake could see her rolling her eyes.

"Got a million of 'em, babe."

"Yes, I know, that's what keeps me up at night."

2

New Year's Eve in Florida.

Not until the orange confetti settled, the bleating plastic horns silenced, and the last party balloon popped, did Reed appreciate the terrible evil that had crept into her life.

It all started with a beautiful night in St. Petersburg to celebrate New Year's Eve. The sky was filled with stars, centerpieced with a bright crescent moon winking like an impish old man. After sunset, the temperature dropped only to seventy degrees. A pleasant breeze coming off Tampa Bay made the tall Canary Island date palms shimmer green and silver in the moonlight.

It was Saturday night, just minutes before ten o'clock.

Reed and Jake arrived at the Hangar, their favorite restaurant in St. Petersburg.

Next door to the Dali Museum and the Mahaffey Theater, the Hangar was aptly named, as it was inside the Albert Whitted Airport Terminal.

With its faux hangar roof, glass walls, and modern floating staircase leading upstairs to the Hangar, the terminal, built in 2007, echoed the atomic architecture of over a half-century ago.

Since the Albert Whitted was a small executive airport, it had only two runways, each less than four-thousand feet long.

So one could enjoy a fried oyster po'boy at the Hangar while watching a Cessna 172 or a Beechcraft G36 Bonanza accelerate down the runway and take flight over the glistening blue-green waters of Tampa Bay.

Reed and Jake might have chosen a table in the main dining room, which featured an old KR-2 single-engine sport airplane hanging from the rafters.

But tonight, the couple preferred the Hangar's Flight Lounge, since they could eat dinner while socializing at the bar.

Wisely, Reed paid five hundred dollars in advance to reserve two seats at the bar on New Year's Eve.

As a bonus, these seats in the Flight Lounge let the couple look out over the main dining room where the Al Downing Tampa Bay Jazz Association was ringing in the New Year with cool sounds of modern jazz.

Reed and Jake approached the bar and spotted two placards marked RESERVED, along with flatware rolled in burgundy cloth napkins, two water goblets, a dish of lime slices, and a chilled bottle of Saratoga sparkling water.

A seasoned bartender, Megan made certain to stand near Reed and Jake's seats as the couple sat down. Jake, of course, held Reed's chair for her.

"Megan, you are the absolute best," Reed said. "Was it difficult holding on to our seats?"

Megan was in her early thirties and came from Ireland, where she had extensive experience bartending in pubs. She wore a black polo shirt, black slacks, and black sneakers. She kept her long auburn hair in a high ponytail. Her freckled pale complexion was luminous. Megan's athletic muscular build suggested she didn't tolerate rudeness or harassment from bar patrons.

"There was a problem or two, Reed, but tweren't nothing this Oirish lass couldn't handle," Megan answered with her Irish brogue stepdancing at full tilt.

"Well, thank you for watching over our seats, Megan," Jake said.

He handed her a hundred-dollar bill.

Megan accepted the tip and smiled warmly at Jake.

She then cracked open the bottle of Saratoga, filled the water goblets, and popped a lime slice in each glass.

Megan didn't bother giving menus to Reed and Jake.

"I know you'll want your usual Hangar wedge salads, but instead of grouper, how about the blackened swordfish? Seriously legend filets came in this morning."

Jake nodded yes to Reed, who answered, "That sounds perfect, Megan."

"Just let me know when I should put in the food order, darlings."

Megan walked away to face the gathering mob of revelers circling her bar.

"Feels as if we're on a lifeboat surrounded by thirsty sharks," Jake said.

"Well, they won't get our Saratoga without a fight, love," Reed said. "Remember, bonk'em on the nose."

Reed and Jake clinked their goblets, then sipped the sparkling mineral water.

The couple wanted to savor this celebration, as both wife and husband were busy people.

In addition to being an attorney as well as a private investigator, Reed co-owned with Jake the nightclub Namaste.

Jake managed Namaste and, since he was a talented pianist, he sometimes played on his Bluthner piano while the performers danced on stage.

He, too, was a licensed private investigator who teamed with Reed to take on complex, sometimes dangerous, cases.

Reed and Jake worked six days a week, leaving Sunday for their lone day of relaxation and recovery.

So yes, they were going to make the most of a rare night out on the town.

Reed dressed accordingly. She wore a silk-chiffon cactus garden print gown. The dress showcased her bare shoulders, narrow waist, and trim figure. She wore three-inch Grand Yeezy heels, bumping her up to average height for a woman. She even wore a bit of make-up, which highlighted her sensational blue eyes, and added a few curls to her shoulder-length blonde hair.

Jake was six-feet tall and weighed a muscular two-hundred pounds. His curly brown hair was kept militantly short. Tonight, he wore a blue plaid suit, an open-collar light blue dress shirt, and black Mephisto sandals.

Reed picked up the scent of Jake's Aqua Di Gio cologne.

"You smell most alluring, my love, so very chypre."

She ran a manicured finger down the length of the blue Saratoga bottle.

Jake watched her with great interest.

"What are you thinking about?"

Reed tapped the tip of his nose.

"I'm thinking how lovely it'll be to start the New Year by making love to you."

Jake set down his water goblet.

"Let's get out of here right now and break every speeding law getting home. If you drive, we'll cross the bay in five minutes."

Reed smiled at her husband.

She gently pinched his left ear lobe, kissed him lightly on his cheek, then whispered in his ear, "No, you impulsive man, we're going to have a bite to eat, listen to some good jazz, then kiss at midnight."

She flicked her tiny tongue in his ear.

"Then we'll go home, and I'll mount my Selle Français stallion."

Before Jake could respond, a woman sitting to Reed's left interjected, "A Selle Français stallion?"

Reed did not give the woman a friendly look.

The woman set down her chalice of Stella Artois beer.

"Sorry, I have freakishly good hearing, and my ears perked up when I heard Selle Français. See, I'm a horse person."

The woman appeared to be in her mid-thirties, close to Reed's age. She kept her black hair in a classic pixie cut with wispy bangs. She had hazel eyes and a round, attractive face. She maybe was five-feet tall. The woman wore a sheer white blouse and a red bra underneath. She completed her evening-out attire with torn blue denims and red leather cowboy boots. She wore no make-up or jewelry, except for a Guess watch.

"And what do you know about the Selle Français?" Reed asked the woman.

"Oooo, getting tested early, I like it!"

She took a gulp of her beer.

"All right, all right, all right. The Selle Français is just about the best show jumper in the world. And they're more than good athletes; they're very smart and have a willing disposition. Why, did you know eleven descendants of the same stallion were Olympians?"

Reed appeared impressed.

"That really is amazing," she said.

Woman has a voice like honey and strawberry lemonade—sweet and tart, Reed thought.

The woman eyeballed Jake, who tried to stay out of the conversation.

"Judging by the looks of your man, I'd say comparing him to a Selle Français was pretty accurate."

Jake looked at the woman with disbelief.

"Excuse me, but what did you just say?" Jake asked the woman.

Reed put her hand on Jake's forearm.

"Don't worry, babe, I got this."

No need for confrontation tonight, she thought. It's New Year's Eve and this woman's probably had a few. And really, I'm supposed to be annoyed she thinks Jake's a stud? Couldn't agree with her more.

Reed smiled confidently at the woman, who returned an equally assured smile.

"Looks to me as if you know your horseflesh," Reed said.

The two women laughed.

"Y'all are aware I'm sitting right here, correct?" Jake asked with a faux pearl clutcher's voice inflection.

Both women laughed again.

3

"How about some introductions," Reed said. "I'm Reed O'Hara. That Selle Français next to me is my husband, Jake Dupree."

The woman extended her hand.

"I'm Raven Doyle, and this big guy over here is *my* stallion, Chance Doyle."

Reed and Raven shook hands.

Chance lifted his bottle of Peroni beer but said nothing. He was an easy six-foot-five and weighed at least two-fifty. Most of it muscle. Black straight hair cut short. Thick black mustache. Bear paws for hands. He wore a white guayabera shirt with black jeans and black cowboy boots tipped with silver.

"Don't let him fool you. Chance can be as talkative as the next drunken Irishman," Raven said.

Chance grinned ever so slightly.

"My man is just checking out the lay of the land," Raven said.

Again, Chance said nothing.

Hmm, wonder who's the alpha here, Chatty Cathy or the Quiet Man, Reed thought.

Chance polished off his beer.

Raven's chalice was empty.

She waved Megan over to her.

Lyle, another bartender, approached Raven instead.

"Nein, nein, nein, I want Megan, not you, bub," Raven said to Lyle, who shrugged and walked away.

Megan took his place.

"There you go, it's the adorable Megan," Raven said. "How about a Stella for me and another Peroni for lunkhead?"

Megan nodded yes. She stole a glance at Raven's breasts, which Raven noticed.

"Hold on, Megan. What can I get for you two, Reed? Maybe something a little stronger than that bougie fizzy water?"

"That's kind of you, Raven, but Jake and I don't drink alcohol, and we're still working on this big bottle of Saratoga."

"I know I should recognize that shade of blue," Raven said, staring at the Saratoga bottle.

Then the Quiet Man spoke.

"Cobalt ... cobalt blue," Chance said.

The Kraken speaks, Jake thought then said, "Impressive, Chance, how did you know that?"

Condescending prig, Chance muttered to himself.

"Well, partner, paint colors are sunburned in my brain from watching all those decorating shows on H Gay TV with my wife."

Megan brought Chance his Peroni and Raven her Stella Artois with a frosty chalice.

She poured the Stella into the chalice, finishing with an inch of foam.

"That's perfect, sweetie, I like a little head with my beer," Raven said.

She winked at Megan, who blushed then returned the wink.

Raven reached over and poked Chance in the ribs. She whispered something to him.

Chance nodded yes.

"Sorry, folks. Chance shouldn't have made that remark about HGTV," Raven said. "Getting him to behave in public is one of the great missions in my life. Shoot, sometimes it's my raisin debtor."

Jake cleared his throat.

"I think you mean ...."

Reed cut him off.

"No worries, Raven. I'm a big proponent of the First Amendment. Speak your mind, as long as you don't yell 'fire' in a crowded theater when there isn't one."

"Preaching to the choir, Reed," Raven said. "I'm just glad Chance is getting over being angry."

"Angry over what, Chance, if you don't mind my asking?" Jake said.

"Don't mind your asking, Jake. Guy earlier asked me why aspirin was white."

"Oh, no."

"Oh, yes. Tried to ignore the drunk, but he insisted on answering his own question: 'Well, you want the aspirin to work don't you?'"

"What a racist jerk," Jake said.

"Yup, just now cooling off."

Chance finished his beer.

He held up the empty bottle.

Megan acknowledged his request for another Peroni.

"Slow down a little, dear husband," Raven said. "I want you to be awake and alert when we get home tonight, if you know what I mean ... and I think you do."

Hey, that's my line, Reed thought.

Chance smiled at Raven. His was a smile that could melt diamonds.

That smile makes me a little tingly, Reed thought.

"Don't fret, Raven. Like I said before, I'm first on the wall and last off it."

"Marines, Chance?" Jake asked.

"Impressive, Jake, how did you know that?"

Well played, Jake thought.

"Your demeanor, your fitness, your haircut. All screams the comportment of a jarhead."

"You're exactly right."

"What'd you do in the Corp?"

"I was an engineer equipment mechanic for four years, then an EOD technician for my second hitch."

"Bravo Zulu. EOF, Explosive Ordnance Disposal, correct?"

"Rah. I'm gonna say you were Army."

"Hooah. Rangers. Squad Advanced Marksman."

"A hunter, eh?"

"Yeah, pretty similar to the Marine Scout Sniper."

"Miss it?"

"Sometimes, but I enjoy being a civilian. And you?"

"I miss it a lot, especially the brothers in my unit."

"I can relate, Chance."

Raven pushed her way into the conversation.

"Enough boring war stories, you manly men. So, Reed, if I may be a smudge bold, why don't you and Jake imbibe? I mean, 'O'Hara' doesn't get more Irish, and we Irish are notorious for drinking 'til the sun comes up and starting all over again."

"Jake never has drank alcohol," Reed said. "But I used to enjoy a beer or two. Nothing like an ice-cold Red Stripe on a Jamaican beach."

"Humpf, never been to Jamaica," Raven said dismissively. "Bit too native for my tastes."

"I don't know how to respond to that, Raven. Anyways, Jake and I own a nightclub in Tampa called Namaste. We help primarily women to recover from their addictions and get a whole new start in life. Since the performers and the staff aren't allowed to drink alcohol, we don't either. It'd be hypocritical of us if we did, right?"

"I suppose so. Namaste ... Namaste ... isn't that a strip bar? At least that's what I've heard."

If an angel shark could smile, she would look like Reed at that moment.

"Namaste is hardly a strip club. If anything, it's an antidote to the strip club virus that spread all over Tampa Bay. In fact, several of our performers once were strippers, enduring the ugly, soul-crushing aspects of that lifestyle."

"Reed, I wasn't saying ...."

"Actually, Raven, you were. No worries. We have allowed performers to dance topless, if they choose. I mean, if it's good enough for the Moulin Rouge, it's good enough for Namaste. But we're about to make a big change at the cabaret."

Raven drank more of her beer.

"Going full nude?"

Reed laughed heartily.

"You, Madame, are an absolute troublemaker. No, we decided, with this new year, there will be no nudity of any sort at Namaste."

Raven almost choked on her Stella.

"What? No more bare bosoms bouncing about in your bar?"

Quick with the alliteration, Jake thought.

"That's right, Raven," Reed said. "Starting out, we wanted an upscale cabaret similar to those in Paris, but Namaste all too often got lumped in with those so-called gentlemen's clubs."

"Let me guess, Amway salesmen and life insurance agents show up, expecting something a little different from what you offer," Raven said.

"Bingo," Jake said.

Raven winked at Jake, which Reed noticed. Jake didn't return the wink.

Megan approached Reed.

"How about I put in your food order—two wedge salads with blackened swordfish, and extra blue cheese dressing for that lash of a husband."

"Lash?" Jake asked.

"Lash is Irish for very attractive," Reed said.

Jake worked up a smug smile.

"Don't let it go to your head, love," Reed said.

"Don't know what you're talking about," he said.

Reed looked over at Raven.

"Have you all eaten yet?"

"No, but we are about to," Raven replied.

"Then let us order you and Chance the blackened swordfish and wedge salads, our treat."

Raven glanced at Chance, who nodded yes.

"That would be lovely of you, Reed, but only if I order you another bottle of the bubbly water."

Megan didn't mind waiting, as she was entranced with Raven.

Wonder if she plays from both sides of the pitch, Megan thought.

"So, did you get all of that, Megan?" Reed asked.

"Yes, darling. I'll get my kitchen working on the four wedgies. I'll bring you and Jake a chilly bottle of Saratoga, Chance a Peroni, and Raven a chaliced Stella with a little head on it."

Raven puckered a kiss to Megan, who returned the gesture.

Duly noted, Reed thought.

Within a couple minutes, in the midst of the chaotic revelry of New Year's Eve, Megan returned with the drink order.

"What do you say we toast the sunset of a good year?" Raven said. "Reed, with you being a lawyer, I bet you could give us a fine toast."

Reed seemed puzzled.

"I never told you I was an attorney, Raven."

"Oh, honey, everyone in Tampa Bay knows you're a lawyer and a private sleuth. It's hardly a well-kept secret around these parts. You couldn't avoid the spotlight even if you tried."

True that, Reed thought.

"Here we go, then," Reed said. "For last year's words belong to last year's language, and next year's words await another voice. And to make an end is to make a beginning."

The foursome lifted their drinks then took polite sips.

"T.S. Eliot," Chance said.

"You are correct, sir." Reed replied enthusiastically.

Chance gave Reed a broad mustached smile, one that was as carnivorous as it was charming.

Reed's face reddened slightly, and she broke Chance's stare by looking down.

So noted, thought Jake.

4

———

"Raven, what do you and Chance do?" Reed asked.

"That's an easy one. We have a horse farm up in Northwest Hillsborough County. My family has owned those four-hundred acres since before the War of Northern Aggression. Carpet baggers are always trying to buy our land so they can develop it into an equestrian estate community. Never gonna happen, guarantee it."

"So you raise horses right in the middle of the urban sprawl?"

"We raise only thoroughbreds. All of them with the proper lineage, of course."

"And she's off," Chance muttered.

Raven playfully slapped his shoulder.

"Whatever, Chance, you know I love this stuff."

"Tell us more, Raven," Jake said. "Reed and I enjoy learning from an authority."

"I don't know how much of an authority I am, but I'll give it a shot."

"Please do," Reed said.

"All right then. First, my philosophy about raising thoroughbreds: there must be blood harmony between sire and mare."

"What do you mean by blood harmony?" Jake asked.

"Purity of the bloodline," Raven said. "No deviation, no adulteration, nothing impure. Our thoroughbreds are champion quality because their lineage goes back to the original Darley Arabian."

"Tell us about this Darley Arabian," Jake said.

"Hah! I could go on for hours about that horse."

"And she has, too," Chance interjected.

This time, Raven slapped his shoulder a little harder.

"Know what, Chance Bartholomew Doyle, you can smooch my hindquarters."

Chance simply smirked.

"In 1704, English gentleman Thomas Darley bought a bay Arabian stallion from Sheik Mirza II of Syria for three-hundred golden sovereigns," Raven said. She paused long enough to stick out her tongue at Chance.

Have to admit, they're kinda adorable, Reed thought.

"By the way, Darley was quite wealthy and a member of Her Majesty's Consult during the reign of Queen Anne. Darley's plan was to import a perfect Arabian stallion to his family's stud farm in England. Which he did. Real sad, though, since Darley died not long after he brought the stallion to England. But that stallion, he lived to be thirty-years-old, and he covered with lots and lots of mares."

"Fascinating, so what was so special about this horse?" Jake asked.

Raven practically radiated with excitement.

"An excellent question, Jake. The Darley Arabian had an abnormally large heart, which gave the stallion much greater strength and stamina. And that's how we ended up with champions like Secretariat and Phar Lap. All about blood harmony, my friend."

Jake lifted his water goblet to Raven.

"I really enjoyed your discourse, Raven. Thank you."

Raven gave him a slight nod, acknowledging the compliment.

"Teacher's pet," Chance said with a devilish smile.

Raven reached over and tousled his black hair.

"Don't go getting jealous on me, my gorgeous horse whisperer."

"You and Chance breed horses together?" Reed asked.

"Yeah, Chance knows almost as much as I do about the horse business since he worked on a ten-thousand-acre cattle ranch in Montaña, owned by Justine and William, right? Isn't Justine an economist and William a bona fide cowboy?"

Chance nodded, "They're a true modern day ranch family."

"Mostly quarter horses in Montaña, Chance?" Reed asked.

"Mostly, but I learned how to ride on the back of a hinny."

Reed's eyes lit up.

"I've ridden on a hinny! Just loved it. So hardy and calm. Tell me if I have this right: a mule is an equine hybrid of a male donkey and a female horse, but a hinny is an offspring of a male horse and a female donkey. Most people wouldn't recognize a hinny because it looks so much like a horse."

"Well done, Reed. Sounds like you've done some riding," Chance said.

He rewarded her with his alluring smile.

There's that tingle again, Reed thought.

"Yes, we've ridden horses in Arizona's Sonoran Desert, up the Blue Mountains in Jamaica, and across cotton fields and through pine forests in Georgia. One of our very favorite rides was galloping on the windward beaches of Aruba on Paso Finos. Really great times."

"Do you still ride?" Raven asked.

"You mean other than Jake?"

Raven, Chance, and Jake broke out in raucous laughter.

"What?" Reed said in a defensive tone. "I can be bawdy when I'm in the mood."

"Are you in the mood now?" Chance asked.

"Just getting warmed up. And no, we rarely ride these days."

Reed reached over to gently pinch Jake's ear lobe.

"After midnight, love," she said.

Yeah, they're pretty cute together, Raven thought.

"Raven, you still ride?" Reed asked.

"Strictly pleasure riding now. On my thoroughbred, Traveller."

"Did you ride competitively?" Jake asked.

"Sure did. Jockeyed several of our thoroughbreds, both amateur and professional level. Won a couple races but got banged up. Now I spend a good portion of my time scouting female jockeys."

"Good for you, Raven," Reed said.

"Never stop advancing, right?" Raven asked.

Reed responded with an enthusiastic thumbs up.

Megan brought the four wedge salads to the two couples.

"Darlings, I made sure the kitchen chose the biggest and best swordfish filets. And that's a honey mustard sauce the chef just whipped up. I added extra bleu cheese dressing for all of you."

"You're so thoughtful, Megan," Raven said. "Be sure to come round when the clock strikes twelve."

She nodded a go-ahead to Chance, who then gave Megan a hundred-dollar bill.

"Thank you so much," she said. "And yes, Raven, I'll come by at midnight."

She m'wahed a kiss to Raven, who pretended the kiss landed on her cheek.

Looks like a budding romance in the works, Reed thought.

For the next fifteen minutes, the couples sat in silence and ate their dinner, appearing to savor each bite of the legend swordfish.

The youthful jazz quartet began playing the 1959 classic "Take Five" by the Dave Brubeck Quartet. The group faithfully followed Brubeck's instrumental version of the jazz song.

Lyle, who had feelings for Megan, knew the lyrics, which he sang under his breath as he mixologized gin and lime juice with a dash of bitters to make a gimlet he called "The Long Goodbye."

Won't you stop and take
A little time with me
Just take five
Stop your busy day and take the time out
To see if I'm alive.

5

———————

The jazz quartet at the Hangar moved seamlessly from Thelonious Monk to Freddie Hubbard to Gerry Mulligan.

Less than an hour from the New Year, the crowd finished eating and wanted only to drink and dance the night away.

Some of the more bibulous revelers fired crepe paper streamers up and over the KR-2 sport plane hanging above them. One man, wearing a black sombrero festooned with red sequins, attempted to land orange and lime slices on the KR-2's wings and fuselage. Augustus Wagram, the Hangar's general manager, persuaded the man to stop throwing fruit at the old plane by offering him an Irish coffee.

"Poor Augustus, the man has to be in his seventies, and there he is talking a drunk off the ledge," Reed said.

"Augie doesn't look American," Chance said.

Sounds rather nativist, Reed thought.

"Augustus is originally from Belgium, and was naturalized over thirty years ago," Reed said.

"Humpf," Chance muttered.

As Megan cleared the plates, she asked, "How were the salads?"

"Simply dee-vine, dahling," Raven said archly.

"Excellent, so another round?"

"Absolutely," Raven answered.

"We're fine, Megan," Reed said, as the quartet shifted from Gerry Mulligan to Miles Davis.

"Gutsy of them to perform Miles Davis," Jake said. "Do you think any of them could buy an adult beverage here?"

"Legally? No way," Reed said.

"Ah youth, so brash and brave, right?" Jake asked.

"True that, love."

"This modern jazz stuff is okay, but I find it too dark and edgy," Raven said.

She lifted her Stella Artois chalice then took a drink as if she were toasting herself for her remark.

"Do you enjoy jazz, Raven?" Jake asked.

She laughed.

"Nope, I'm strictly a bluegrass and country music girl," she said sarcastically. "Of course I like jazz, Jakey, mostly the big bands of the forties."

"Count Basie?" Jake inquired.

"No, Glenn Miller."

"Duke Ellington?"

Raven shook her head no.

"Tommy Dorsey."

"How about Cab Calloway?"

"Ha! Why take a cab when you can ride in a limo? Benny Goodman was the zoot suited king of swing, don't ya know. 'Sing, Sing, Sing' is my all-time favorite song. That el Spanish-o dude Louis Prima wrote the song, but Benny baby made it come alive. And Gene Krupa, his drum solo on that very song elevated drummers from line accompanists to important solo voices in a band."

"So we have Gene Krupa to thank for those interminable drum solos at rock concerts?" Reed asked.

"Yupper puppers," Raven answered.

"Again, I am impressed, Raven," Jake said.

"I do my homework, Professor."

"A single point deduction regarding Benny's threads. He wore a jazzy tux: a green three-piece suit, an ecru jacket over forest green pants—but never ever a zoot suit."

Raven tilted back her head and laughed loudly.

"Well smack my buns and call me Sally. I knew you were up on your music history, just not *that* up, Jake."

Hmm, how exactly did she know that Jake was a music history buff? Reed wondered. Are we getting led down a rabbit hole?

The jazz quartet stopped playing. Crowd noise, fueled by all manner of premium liquor, registered higher and higher on the sound level meter.

Microphone in hand, Augustus addressed the celebrants.

"Please, if I may have your attention, everyone. Let's quiet down only a little bit, please. The time is near for the New Year. At my signal, let's count down together, then all of us sing 'Auld Lang Syne'."

An elderly man, wearing a red cardboard top hat, a bright yellow aloha shirt covered with pink hibiscus blooms, white Bermuda shorts, and Birkenstocks with yellow knee-high socks, suddenly jumped on his chair.

"I like your plan, Auggie," he yelled in a hoarse voice. "Let's storm the beaches and hit those Krauts with all we got."

The crowd roared its approval. The man waved both arms and attempted to dance a jig. Fortunately, two servers persuaded him to step down from his chair.

Only in America, Augustus thought.

Only in Florida, Reed opined to herself.

Looks like St. Pete is still God's Waiting Room, Raven thought.

"Time for the countdown, everyone," Augustus announced. "All together now ... ten ... nine ... eight ... seven ... six ... five ... four ... three ... two ... one ... now: Happy New Year!"

Everyone yelled "Happy New Year!" back at Augustus, then followed with the obligatory hugs and kisses.

Some openly wept, while others chugged from bottles of Champagne.

Mr. Pink Hibiscus wrapped his spindly arms around a young female server who gently pushed away the old man when he attempted to kiss her.

"But I took a little blue pill, sweetie, I'm ready to gallop," he yelled at the woman.

Then he neighed like a horse.

The woman put her hands on her hips.

"Mr. Ed, I don't care if you took ten Viagra pills, I'm not going to kiss you, New Year or not, so go away."

The man walked away while yelling "Elderly abuse, elderly abuse...neigh!"

Meanwhile, the jazz quartet backed Augustus as he began singing "Auld Lang Syne."

The raucous crowd joined him:

Should auld acquaintance be forgot
And never brought to mind?
Should auld acquaintance be forgot
And days of auld long syne?
For auld lang syne, my dear,
For auld lang syne
We'll take a cup of kindness yet
For days of auld lang syne.

Raven and Chance had just kissed and hugged when Megan came up to them.

"Happy New Year, Raven."

Raven let go of Chance and turned toward Megan.

"You're pure Irish beauty, love. Happy New Year to you. May there be no tears, only treasure. Now come here and give your auntie a big kiss."

Megan smiled, then gave Raven a kiss that started out reserved then quickly turned passionate. Their embrace lasted a good thirty seconds.

Jake and Reed were nonplussed, though Chance had no reaction.

Suddenly, Mr. Pink Hibiscus elbowed his way up to Raven and Megan, who still were kissing.

"Now that's what I'm talking about! Nothing like seeing two broads swapping spit."

Chance deftly moved between the man and the two women.

"Old timer, either walk away right now or I'll break you up into kindling."

The man made the wise choice of scampering away to find someone else to bother.

Chance shook his head in disdain.

"That boy is gonna be lucky to make it through the first day of the New Year,"

"I think you're right, but I swear I've seen that guy somewhere before," Jake said.

He gathered Reed into his arms.

The couple stared into each other's eyes.

They were oblivious to the madding crowd swirling around them.

Reed stood on her toes to kiss her husband.

Theirs was a kiss replete with passion and purpose, an expression of love supreme.

"You know, my Reed, Ingrid Bergman said a kiss is a lovely trick nature designed to stop speech when words are superfluous."

Reed giggled.

"Well then, stop talking so much and kiss me again, my sweet Jake."

Sweet Jake complied.

6

———

Reed wanted to speak with Raven, but she and Megan were still huddled.

Raven hugged Megan as she softly whispered something to her. Megan nodded yes and whispered back to her. The two exchanged winks.

"Alas, all of you, time for me to get back behind the bar," Megan announced before walking away.

Reed approached Raven.

"Can we chat?"

Raven's face was flushed and she appeared out of breath.

"Of course, what's up?"

"I was wondering if you and Chance would like to try out Namaste one night this week."

Raven pretended to ponder the invite.

"Hmm, let's see, I'll have to check my social calendar ... just messing with you, Reedley. We'd love to experience Namaste."

"How about Friday night, then?"

"That's so weird: I was thinking about Chance and me going to Namaste this Friday night! Great minds, you know."

Interesting, she had already planned to visit Namaste, Reed thought. This gets more intriguing by the minute.

"We'll reserve you and Chance a front-row table. The club doesn't get jumping until about nine, so how about you all come by then?"

"Nine is sublime. Sounds like a plan, Stan."

Raven was slightly wobbly.

Reed put her hand on Raven's shoulder.

"You okay?"

"Just fine, but I think I'm done drinking for the night. Those Stellas kick my butt every time."

"Is Chance going to drive?"

"Yes, Mom, he's good to go for driving home."

"You know how I worry about you, Daughter Dearest."

"Hah! You got a pretty good sense of humor for a highfalutin lawyer type."

Reed paused then said, "Better to be funny than phony."

Raven looked puzzled.

"Can't make hide nor hair of that. Think I'll figure out that assphorism in the morning when I'm sober."

Assphorism, let it go, Reed thought.

"Jake and I are heading out, Raven. If we leave now, we'll get a head start on the folks going home once the bars close."

"So practical and levelheaded. Really kind of annoying. And we were just starting to have fun."

Raven pouted.

"Now, now, all good things, and bad for that matter, must come to an end. How about we get together for lunch this week?"

Raven transformed into a shiny happy person.

"What a great idea, girly girl. Here, take my card. Gots my digits on it."

She reached into her back pocket and pulled out a business card, which she handed to Reed, who looked carefully at the blood red card.

"Hmm, are you a professional dominatrix, 'Miss Ravenous'?"

Raven made a perfect "O" with her mouth.

"What the heck! Gave ya the wrong card. Anyways, it has my phone number on it. And no, bondage is only a hobby of mine."

"Probably a little more fun than jigsaw puzzles?"

"Yeah, a smudge more fun."

It's a *smidge*, goodness, is she doing this on purpose or is she just a yahoo, Reed asked herself.

As if on telepathic cue, Jake and Chance walked up and stood next to their respective spouses.

"Time to hit the road, Chance," Jake said.

"Expect we will meet up again further down the road."

The two men shook hands, the grips firm yet not trying to crush a fistful of gravel.

"Give me a call, sweet Reed." Raven said.

"Will do."

They hugged goodbye. Raven lingered, attempting to slide her right-hand down Reed's derriere.

"That's a mission impossible, Raven," Reed said, as she broke from the hug.

Raven shrugged.

"Can't blame Polly Amorous for trying."

While holding hands, Reed and Jake walked down the Hangar's floating staircase and out into the New Year's night.

"Give them five minutes, then we'll leave," Raven said.

"Rah," Chance answered.

The New Year's celebration showed no signs of winding down. The jazz quartet kept playing, barely pausing between songs. Some couples slow-danced, while others sat at their tables and nuzzled. Megan and her partner Lyle stalwartly attempted to fill drink orders while cutting off the drunk and disorderly. Realizing the Hangar was in for a profitable night, while not once having to call in the local constabulary, GM Augustus Wagram ambled with quiet joy through the raucous crowd.

Even Mr. Pink Hibiscus established a beachhead of sorts. An attractive brunette in a revealing gold sequined gown led Mr. Pink Hibiscus by the hand through the restaurant. A good six-inches taller than he and at least 30 years younger, the woman wore a thousand-yard stare. She also wore his Rolex on her left wrist.

"Still a player, ya clod hoppers," Mr. Pink Hibiscus yelled.

Though most people ignored him, one obviously envious man muttered to his wife, "More like a *payer*, that's a solid gold Rolex she's wearing. Look, Thelma, she's listing portside."

Thelma smiled lovingly at her husband.

"Harry Balzac, let the man enjoy the time he has left on this earth. Besides, his watch coordinates nicely with her dress."

Harry looked admiringly at his wife.

"Thelma Balzac, you are a good and fine woman. Happy New Year, my dear."

The Balzacs kissed.

"Ain't that sweet as blackstrap molasses," Chance said. "What do you say we get out of this sugar factory, Raven."

"Let's go, boo. Gonna need an insulin shot if we stay here much longer."

As Raven and Chance walked out of the Hangar, Augustus wished them a safe drive home. The couple completely ignored him.

Once out in the parking lot, Raven slid her small hand down the back of Chance's jeans.

"Nice touch with the white aspirin joke, hubby."

Chance tipped his imaginary Stetson.

"Thank you kindly, ma'am. And I'll try not to blast one while you're keeping your hand warm on my butt."

"You better not, Chance Doyle. Your farts are worse than Traveller's."

"I'll keep a cork in it. Promise. So what'd you think of Reed O'Hara?"

"She's a tough little scrapper, but I think we'll manage her just fine and dandy."

"Oh, you got this, Raven. And what's up with that Irish hottie?"

"Megan's coming by after she breaks down the bar. Probably be around four in the morning."

"Four? Don't know if I can stay awake that long."

Raven laughed.

"Honey bear, no boys allowed tonight. Just get your handsome self a good night's rest. Megan and I will keep ourselves occupied."

7

Despite Reed ignoring every speed-limit sign between St. Petersburg and Tampa, she and Jake didn't make it back to their downtown penthouse apartment until well past two a.m.

It had been a pleasant drive across Tampa Bay on the Howard Frankland Bridge. Riding shotgun, Jake spotted the dome of Tropicana Field, home ballpark for the Tampa Bay Rays. The Trop's dome lit up a bright orange whenever the Rays won a baseball game; in honor of the New Year, the Trop shone like a huge Day-Glo navel orange. With no cloud cover, moonlight partnered with stiff winds from the Gulf of Mexico to make the bay waters shake and shimmy in a way that'd make any belly dancer proud.

Off to the east, the impressive Tampa skyline glowed with promise and possibilities.

"There's no place like home," Jake said in a hushed voice.

"Got that right," Reed said as she shifted into high gear and roared down the bridge's passing lane in her black Mustang GT.

When she and Jake walked into their apartment, Reed instructed Echo's Alexa to turn on only the accent lights, then to open the tall beige drapes in the living room. The drapes parted like theater curtains, and the floor-to-ceiling windows showcased a grand view of the downtown skyline, Harbour Island, and wide-mouth Tampa Bay feeding out into the Gulf of Mexico. She took off her heels and rubbed her feet.

"Oh, no you don't, Reed O'Hara," Jake exclaimed from the kitchen, where he was preparing herbal tea for the two of them. "Massaging your feet is my job!"

Reed quietly giggled.

Works every time, she thought.

"How's that tea coming along, bub?"

"Just needs to steep, love."

Reed had Alexa play music by jazz trumpeter Cindy Bradley. The first song was "Prelude". Bradley's solo trumpet play moved dreamily around the foundational theme. Her trumpet was wistful, controlled, and ethereal. "Prelude" was a sort of backstage warm-up for Bradley. The song concluded with the trumpeter's heels tapping rhythmically on her way to center stage before a lively audience.

"Such brilliant music," Reed said.

Jake came into the living room with two steamy mugs of Raspberry Zinger tea. He handed a mug to his wife, then joined her on the sofa.

"Totally agree, Bradley has impressive range," Jake replied. "She can start with head-on bebop, then shift to funk and R&B and contemporary jazz."

Reed blew on her mug of tea, took a cautious sip, then put her feet on Jake's lap.

"If you massage my feeties, I'll gladly listen to your telling me more about Bradley."

Jake sat his mug on the end table.

"You have a deal, my love."

He first tended to Reed's soles, running a thumb across the length of each arch.

"Cindy Bradley's from Buffalo," said in a tweed-jacket-with-patches professorial tone. "She has a B.A. from Ithaca College in jazz studies and music education, and a master's in jazz trumpet performance from the New England Conservatory."

Jake massaged each heel, applying just the right amount of pressure.

"Oooh, Jake, if I had any state secrets, I'd tell them all to you right now."

Reed tilted her head back and closed her eyes.

"Didn't you mention that Bradley is very community minded?" she said in almost a whisper.

Jake moved on to Reed's toes. He'd readily admit, with no sense of shame, that he had a slight fetish for Reed's feet. He was especially obsessed with her teeny tiny toes.

"Only the toes knows, my little pretty."

"Jacob Jordan Dupree, stop being weird."

"Yes, ma'am. Sorry. You asked about Cindy Bradley's civic minded-ness, right?"

"Yes, yes, I did."

"Well, let me tell you, Bradley has put on dozens and dozens of jazz workshops at high schools and community colleges all over the country."

"What an amazing artist. And it's great to see a female instrumen-talist breaking into the male-centric jazz world."

"Amen."

Jake patted her feet.

"All done, hon."

"Thank you, my sweet and slightly odd husband."

Bradley's "Massive Transit" started up.

"Great song," Reed said. "I think I enjoy music much more when I know something about the musician."

"Preaching to the choir, my intel-delectable."

"Is that even a word?"

"Sure, why not. A new word for the new year."

Reed drank more of her raspberry tea.

"Such a superb night at the Hangar, wasn't it?"

Jake drank some tea as well.

"Flugelhorn."

"What?"

"Flugelhorn. Bradley also plays the flugelhorn. It's a fun word to say. Flugelhorn. Rolls across your tongue."

"Flugelhorn. Kind of tickles my mouth when I say it."

"Such a good sport. Yes, the Hangar was a lot of fun. And quite interesting. What do you make of Raven and Chance Doyle?"

Reed finished her tea. Her intention in responding to Jake was to be plain spoken without being alarmist.

"Felt like a Dixie drive-by, really. They're pleasant enough, but I can't see how we could be friends. We'll host them at Namaste on Friday night, and that will do it for me, at least socially. I want to find out what Raven is up to, though, so I'll have lunch with her one day this week."

Jake finished his tea.

"We're going to try hibiscus tea tomorrow. And I agree with you. The Doyles are pure trouble. Raven tried entirely too hard to send out white supremacist feelers. You know, all that blood harmony drivel. And Chance being offended by the white aspirin joke—he was just laying down cover for his wife."

Reed nodded in agreement then said, "And how about these annoying tidbits: Raven named her horse after Robert E. Lee's horse, Traveller; she called the Civil War the 'War of Northern Aggression'; she thinks Jamaica is too native for her. I mean, for goodness' sake."

"She also described modern jazz, which is dominated by Black musicians, as dark and angry. Did you catch the little game she played with big band leaders?"

Reed appeared puzzled.

"I didn't catch that. Tell me more."

"Each time I mentioned a Black big band leader, she countered with a white band leader."

"Hmm, interesting for sure. Do you get the feeling she wanted us to pick up on her racism? Maybe she counted on us rejecting her overtures."

"Not sure I follow."

"Okay, maybe she wasn't recruiting us. She was challenging us."

"Might be onto something, Reed. I bet you picked up on Raven knowing quite a bit about us."

"I did. I challenged her on it, and she deflected like a pro."

"Was tonight her opening gambit, then?"

"I think it was, Jake"

"So what's her end game?"

"I don't know, but I'll guarantee it isn't good. I'm not going to wait until Friday. Time to be proactive, for sure."

"I know exactly what that means."

"Oh really? Do tell."

"You're letting Ravel off the front porch."

"Yes I am, but don't let Ravel catch you comparing her to a bloodhound."

Jake laughed.

"Thanks for the heads up, love."

"You are most welcome."

Reed leaned over and kissed Jake passionately.

"Wow, what was that for?"

Reed smiled alluringly.

"Just a reminder—I'm going to keep the promise I made to you earlier tonight."

Jake was about to speak when Reed put her index finger on his lips.

"No, my love, no silly puns about horsing around or saddling up."

Jake laughed.

"How about, I'm really feeling my oats right now?"

"Absolutely not."

Reed rose from the sofa.

She walked toward the master bedroom. As usual, she left her shoes exactly where she took them off. Reed stood in the bedroom doorway. A single bedside lamp illuminated her. She gently tugged at her dress, which fell around her feet.

She wore neither a bra nor panties.

For only a few moments, Reed remained in the doorway, her back to Jake, her head poised over her left shoulder.

She was a living, breathing Rodin sculpture.

Reed then walked into the bedroom.

Jake gathered up her shoes, then her dress, then trotted to the bedroom and closed the door behind them.

8

———————

It was exactly four a.m. as Andre entered La Mesa, an all-night diner on Columbus Avenue in West Tampa.

Jake had suggested La Mesa to Andre, who was head of security at Namaste.

"I love that place," Jake said. "Reminds me of Mallorca's in Old San Juan."

The mostly Hispanic hangout featured a horseshoe-shaped island countertop, Alaskan chilly AC, bright fluorescent lighting, and large glass windows. Local gringos loved coming to La Mesa to get a hearty meal after a long night of clubbing. It was common to see a very tough Guatemalan having a pleasant talk with a young white couple from South Tampa. They managed to communicate through broken English and even more fractured Spanish. There was an unspoken understanding that people were to get along. As a result, there hadn't been a fight of any import for over fifteen years. Weapons were to be left in cars. Bad attitudes were to be checked at the door. La Mesa was a sanctuary of relative peace and harmony.

Andre had closed down Namaste thirty minutes ago.

It was a good night at the nightclub with no incidents at all.

Namaste always closed on New Year's Day, so Andre had the next thirty-six hours all to himself, and his first stop would be the Cuban diner. Normally, he ordered grilled flank steak and onions with yellow rice and fried sweet plantains at La Mesa. But on this late night, where the shining crescent moon toggled the tides of Tampa Bay, he had no intention of having his usual fare.

Rather, he wanted to enjoy a café con leche, a lusty combination of expresso and hot milk, and good conversation with his brother, Vlad. After his eyes adjusted to the bullying fluorescent light, Andre spotted his brother sitting on the side of the island countertop. A gregarious man, Vlad was talking with people around him. He spoke both in English and in Spanish. Vlad had reserved the chrome swivel stool to his right for Andre by placing a café con leche, a small blue plastic glass of ice water, and toasted Cuban bread on the counter in front of the stool. Andre watched Vlad laugh uproariously over a comment made by a viejo to his left.

Then Vlad saw Andre.

He practically leapt off his stool.

"As-salamu alaykum, my brother."

Andre gave Vlad a smile as broad as the Grand Canyon.

"And peace be unto you, my dear brother."

They shook hands vigorously.

"Please, Andre, do sit down. You have some catching up to do. I'm on my second coffee!"

At six-foot, six-inches tall and weighing two-hundred sixty pounds, Vlad was slightly larger than his older brother. Both men shared an African American father and a Russian mother. Both men were college educated and valued intellect over physicality. Both men were deeply spiritual, Vlad through his Muslim faith, Andre through Buddhism. And both men were single, though open to a committed relationship with the right woman.

Andre sipped his café con leche. He didn't care that it was lukewarm.

He dipped the Cuban toast into his coffee, then bit into the delicious soggy toast.

"Remember when Momma fixed us hot chocolate in the morning and let us dunk our toast?"

"I do, Andre. Such a sweet time in our life."

"I miss Mother and Father so much, Vlad. One day, we need to shelve our busy lives and visit them for an entire month in Stockholm."

"A lovely dream, brother, but I don't see that happening any time soon."

"Can't get away from those financial algorithms?"

Vlad was a respected analyst in the equity, bond, and commodities markets.

It was a testament to his intelligence and acumen that the financial house looked beyond his youth and his being a Black Muslim to hire him.

"No more than you can stop keeping Namaste and Reed O'Hara safe."

Protecting Reed O'Hara was not part of Andre's official job description. It just came naturally that he would become her bodyguard. However, Reed was hardly a delicate damsel in distress: she was an expert in firearms use and held a black belt in tae kwon do. She also had Jake. But Andre didn't differentiate between Namaste and Reed. It was one world in his eyes, and he was the ever-vigilant gatekeeper.

"Well played, Vlad. You're right, as usual. I cannot see myself being away from here for that long. What Reed and Jake are doing ruffles some feathers. And I won't let anything bad happen to the wonderful people at Namaste. Some of the women have had such horrible lives. They're all getting better, at their own individual pace. It's almost my sacred duty to protect them, all of them."

Vlad lifted his coffee cup to Andre.

"You are a good man, Andre. I admire your dedication."

Both men finished their coffee and toast, then ordered two more cups of café con leche.

"Plan on sleeping tonight, baby bro?"

"No worries, I can drink coffee all day long and sleep like a sultan."

"Ah, youth."

"Really, Andre? You're only three years older than I."

Andre grinned mischievously.

"Yes, older ... and wiser ... and better looking."

"You are in exceptionally good spirits tonight. Hmm, is thou perchance in love, dear brother?"

Andre laughed the laugh of the justly accused.

"I won't admit just yet to being in love, but I confess that I'm smitten."

Vlad put his hand on Andre's shoulder.

"I am so happy for you. And you deserve the kind of happiness only a woman can bring into your life."

"Though he's a despicable human being, Woody Allen was right about one thing: women are all we know of paradise on earth," Andre replied.

"So, who is she? Please tell me that she is not one of the fallen women of Namaste."

Andre gave Vlad a severe look.

"I try not to judge people, even when my brother makes an inappropriate comment. We are all fallen, Vlad. We are all imperfect. We are all a work in progress. A person's past doesn't matter to me. I neither condemn nor absolve someone else's so-called sins. Put simply, it is what is."

The elderly waiter brought them two piping hot cups of café con leche.

"Gracias, señor," Vlad said.

"De nada," the old man said in a raspy voice.

The brothers sat in silence, blowing on their coffee and sipping carefully.

Perhaps I never have had an unspoken thought, Vlad admitted to himself.

"I deserved your taking me to the woodshed," the younger brother said.

Andre winced.

"I don't know why, but I'm not comfortable with that expression. I'm sorry for snapping at you, Vlad. The woman's name is Chenoa. She's an assistant to Reed in private investigations."

Vlad raised his eyebrows, though didn't say a word.

"I know, I know, workplace romances are tricky at best."

Suddenly, an argument broke out between two young Hispanic men across from them.

Off in the far corner, an extremely large Hispanic man sat at a card table. He looked up from his *La Gaceta* newspaper and took note of the argument that escalated rapidly. The man's name was Montaña. And he was a mountain of a human being, standing six-feet, nine-inches tall and weighing four-hundred pounds, when he dieted. Montaña's arrangement with La Mesa was he could eat and drink for free as long as he provided security. While it seemed a losing proposition for the diner at first blush, Montaña's presence alone had a quieting effect.

Montaña set down his newspaper, finished his coffee, and rose like an awakened leviathan. He ambled over to the argument that was getting louder by the second. The two men sat next to each other at the counter. Montaña walked up behind them, putting one mano grande on the man to his right, the other mano grande resting on the man to his left.

"Tranquilo."

That was all he said.

The two men stopped arguing, then nodded respectfully to Montaña.

They knew he could pop their heads like a couple of annoying pimples.

"Los manos, ahora," Montaña ordered.

The men shook hands.

"Bien, no más, sí?"

They quickly said together, "Sí, sí, sí, señor."

Montaña ambled back to his card table.

A waiter already had brought him a large plate of ropas viejas with white rice and four blue plastic glasses of ice water.

Montaña resumed reading *La Gaceta* while taking surprisingly dainty bites of shredded roast pork that really did resemble ropas viejas, or old clothes.

"Impressive, isn't it?" Vlad said.

"Sure is, such economy of speech and movement. I really admire Man Mountain Miguel."

"Don't you mean Gran Montaña?"

"Or Big Tony Montaña."

"A *Scarface* reference, excellent! How about El Grande y El Alto?"

Montaña looked up from his newspaper.

"Mira, no más."

He gave a slight wink to Andre and Vlad.

Both brothers nodded respectively to Two-Ton Tony.

"Man has freakish hearing," Vlad whispered.

"Certainly does, hermanito."

Vlad chuckled.

"Somehow 'hermanito' sounds loftier than 'baby brother'."

"I agree."

"Please tell me about She-no-a, that's how you pronounce her name, right?"

Andre nodded yes.

"Chenoa is brilliant and educated and beautiful. She has the soul of an angel. When she was a nun, she colored her long hair a bright fuchsia with black tips. But she has let her natural red hair grow out, and it's stunning. Kind of takes my breath away."

"Whoa, hold on there, Andre. Did you just try to slip by me that Chenoa was a nun?"

Andre smiled.

"I didn't think you would miss that. Yes, Chenoa renounced her vows a couple years ago. Reed hired her first as a factotum, then Chenoa moved up to investigative assistant. She has her PI license. I taught her proper firearm use and safety. She's a fast learner, that woman."

"So, she's a nun noir," Vlad said.

He appeared quite pleased with himself.

"Clever to a fault line, brother. But Chenoa isn't a nun anymore, and she's hardly a dark individual."

"All right, fine, but 'nun noir' sorta works."

Guess I'll toss this puppy a bone, Andre thought.

"Sure, it sorta works, and it's pretty darn funny."

Vlad positively beamed.

"Why thank you, oh wise elder. Back to Chenoa. Would you say you two are falling in love?"

Andre polished off his second cafe con leche.

He ruminated for about a minute.

"We might be, Vlad. We know we like each other. A lot."

Vlad again put his hand on Andre's shoulder.

"I am so happy for you. I truly am. I can't wait to be an uncle."

Andre laughed so loudly, Montaña looked up from his newspaper.

Andre held up both hands in surrender.

Montaña smiled. Sort of.

"Let's not get ahead of ourselves, okay?"

"Fair enough. Well, my dear brother, it's time for me to go home and get a few hours of sleep."

Andre frowned.

"Are you working on New Year's Day?"

"Only for the afternoon. The markets never sleep; even when they are closed, there's plenty of backroom maneuvers to watch."

"Do you ever consider yourself a very talented bookie?"

This time, Vlad laughed, though he muffled his laugh in deference to Montaña.

"You're not the first person to ask me that question. Off the record, there are an awful lot of similarities between the two professions."

"High risk, high reward, for instance?"

"Or low risk, low reward. It's all about the client's comfort zone."

"Okay, but don't work yourself into the ground, Vlad."

"I promise, I won't. Goodbye, dear brother."

The two men stood and bear hugged.

Andre sat back down as Vlad left the coffee shop.

"Señor, un más café, por favor."

The old Hispanic gentleman simply nodded.

My ego remains too strong, all we talked about was me, Andre thought.

He grimaced in shame.

The viejo brought him his coffee.

"Con paz, con paz, mí amigo," the man said in a soothing voice.

He smiled with a twinkle in his dark brown eyes.

"Do not borrow the trouble, el jefe ... soon come all on its own, si?" the viejo asked.

"Yes, gracias, señor," Andre replied.

He poured a tiny waterfall of sugar in his last café con leche.

Since the coffee cups at La Mesa were plastic, Andre was denied the pleasant sound of a metal spoon clinking against a china mug. He took a sip of his coffee then happened to look out at La Mesa's parking lot. Vlad was almost to his silver BMW when a white Ford Explorer suddenly pulled up in front of him.

Vlad stopped walking. He appeared confused.

The takedown of Vlad took mere seconds.

Four white men in black face scrambled out of the Explorer.

They moved with the speed and agility of a NASCAR pit crew.

One man put up the hatch of the SUV and remained there.

Another man walked quickly up to Vlad and electroshocked him with a stun gun.

Vlad immediately dropped to the ground.

The man spun around, ran to the Explorer, and got in behind the wheel.

Two other men rushed to Vlad, placed zip cuffs on his hands and feet, then carried him to the rear of the SUV.

They carelessly tossed him into the cargo bed as if he were no more than a sack of oats.

After closing the hatch, the three men jumped into the Explorer, which blasted out of La Mesa's parking lot and sped east on Columbus Avenue.

There was nothing Andre could do—the crew simply moved too fast.

He had jumped off his stool and ran out to the parking lot.

He reached inside his sport coat and realized his Desert Eagle .50 caliber pistol was locked away in his truck.

Horrified, he could only watch as the Explorer grew smaller and smaller before disappearing altogether in the black night.

"Oh. Dear Lord, they took my beautiful baby brother."

9

———————

Ten a.m. on New Year's Day.

Reed and Jake remained sound asleep in their master bedroom. They had turned off their phones, tablets, and laptops, with the plan to snare at least a few hours of uninterrupted sleep. Sated from their love making, they had fallen asleep with Reed resting her head on Jake's shoulder. As was her nightly habit, Reed had pulled her beloved eiderdown duvet over her head. Truly, theirs was a scene of intimate repose. Alas, even Reed and Jake's plans sometimes go awry: the front doorbell rang like a car alarm with Tourette's.

What in the world, how did someone get by our security system? Reed wondered with only one blue eye open.

The easiest way to reach their penthouse was by the elevator, which required a code to reach the top floor. Of course, there was a thirty-three-floor emergency stairwell, which also required a passcode to enter the penthouse hallway.

Reed carefully got out of bed, as she didn't want to awaken Jake.

She gazed at her husband, who was on his back, his hands folded across his chest, and his right leg sticking out from under the duvet. A considerate man to a fault, Jake snored ever so diplomatically.

Goodness, I do so love that man, Reed declared to herself.

She put on the red silk pajamas that Jake gave her for Christmas.

Reed had given Jake an empty gift box on Christmas morning.

"Those are invisible pajamas—just the way I like it," Reed said playfully to Jake.

Then she gave him a fob to an infinite black metallic Lincoln Navigator.

"Exactly what I asked for in my letter to Santa!" Jake exclaimed.

Reed padded quietly out of the bedroom and made a beeline to the massive oak front door.

She checked the video feed from the security camera in the hallway.

There was Ravel, grinning like the Joker at the security camera.

That woman so loves messing with me, Reed thought.

Chenoa stood behind Ravel. Her arms were folded. She tapped her right foot. She didn't appear at all happy.

Two bulging Alessi Bakery bags sat on the hallway floor.

"Beware of geeks bearing gifts, sweetie pie," Ravel said to the security camera.

"Speak for yourself, Ravel," Chenoa said.

Ravel glared at Chenoa.

"Enough of your nunsense, you refuse to appreciate my play on words."

"Oh, I get it. I just don't like being described as a geek. I'm not. At all. Besides, the expression is 'Timeo Danaos et dona ferentes' or 'I fear the Danaans, even when they bear gifts.' FYI, dear Ravel, Danaans were ancient Greeks."

Chenoa was well versed in Latin after attending Catholic parochial school, Loyola University Chicago, and completing her training to become a nun at the Convent of St. Anne's.

"Well, la dee da, Chenoa," Ravel said.

Reed had heard enough: she buzzed open the front door.

It's like Cain and Abel cross-stitched with Lewis and Martin, she thought.

Ravel strutted inside the apartment, with Chenoa holding up the rear—as well as the Alessi bags.

"Surprise, Reed, we couldn't resist celebrating New Year's Day with you," she said.

Ravel was a true enigma. Raised by loving and dedicated parents in Montreux, Switzerland, she learned to read and write by her third birthday. Her parents gave her a MacBook a year later. She scored 152, genius level, on the Stanford-Binet intelligence quotient test.

But Ravel was a rebel through and through. At thirteen, she forsook days of honey and edelweiss for nights of ecstasy-laced raves, hookah lounges, and tawdry trysts with equally rebellious girls.

Out of sheer frustration with their alt daughter and motivated by a growing fear that they could lose her, Ravel's parents enrolled her in Surval Montreux, one of Switzerland's premier boarding schools for girls. This way, her parents reasoned, Ravel would be in a protected environment while still being close to home.

Ravel actually enjoyed Surval Montreux: she was challenged intellectually and had one girlfriend after another.

Then she met Riley from Miami. Riley was intelligent enough for Ravel, yet it was her freakish attitude toward life that was most attractive to Ravel.

They were known as "The Twins" at Surval. Both were five-feet tall and strikingly beautiful. They both wore their black hair short; the teens refused to wear makeup or jewelry. The easiest way to tell them apart was Riley's eyes were emerald green, Ravel's a crystal purple persuasion.

Now seventeen, Ravel was completely in love with Riley, who felt the same way toward Ravel.

When Riley asked Ravel to leave Surval and come live in Miami with her family, Ravel immediately accepted.

Despite vehement protests from her parents, Ravel crossed the Atlantic with her true love. When the plane touched down at Miami International Airport, the teens celebrated with a kiss in first class.

Alas, the romance did not have a happy ending. Riley's parents wouldn't allow Ravel to stay with them, mumbling something about "lesbian eurotrash."

Riley's father at least gave Ravel five-hundred dollars and a ticket on a Trailways bus to Tampa.

"You'll fit in better in the armpit of the Gulf," he told Ravel.

She glommed onto Tampa Bay's over-the-top underworld like an Entlebucher Mountain puppy taking to her mother's teat. An epicenter of the Marilyn Manson-inspired Goth lifestyle, Tampa especially appealed to Ravel. She spent countless nights at El Castillo in Ybor City, engaging in one sexual encounter with a woman after another—the women often gave her money just so she could eat at a lousy restaurant and stay at an even lousier motel.

Addicted to crack cocaine and methamphetamine, Ravel was on her way to an early urn. Then Reed O'Hara came into her life. Ravel had heard through the alt vine that Reed sometimes helped women in trouble. After an interview of sorts at Namaste, Reed, sensing Ravel's high potential, offered her a position as assistant office manager. But there were riders attached: Ravel had to enter rehab, get clean and sober, and never again use narcotics.

Ravel overcame her addictions with Swiss precision and determination. Within three months, she was working full-time at Namaste. She was healthy, content, and centered. And she never forgot that Reed saved her life.

"I don't understand, Ravel, you figured out the passcodes to the elevator and to our front door," Reed said. "Why didn't you just let yourself in—you've done it before, plenty of times."

Ravel smiled jauntily.

"Reed darling, I didn't want to barge in on you two doing the wild thing—I swear, y'all can be like a couple of bunny rabbits."

Don't entirely disagree with her on that count, Reed thought.

"You didn't interrupt us, but we *were* trying to sleep. And lower your voice, Jake is still resting."

"Yes, ma'am," Ravel whispered.

Chenoa set the bags on the kitchen island and got out the boxes bearing the Alessi logo of a chef wearing an oversized toque blanche and whistling while he kneaded dough. The grand panaderia of West Tampa since 1912, Alessi Bakery was known for its pastries and breads, as well as the roast pork, picadillo, and chicken combo, bruschetta, deviled crabs, shrimp and scallop empanadas, and chicken pot pies made from scratch. Chenoa arranged the pastries on white scalloped stoneware plates. She plated mini mousse cream pies, tiny eclairs and cream puffs, cannoli, black and white cookies, and chocolate-dipped strawberries.

"Such a gorgeous arrangement, Chenoa," Reed said. "Ravel, please get the bowl of sliced melon out of the fridge. I'll fix us some coffee, okay?"

Ravel saluted Reed, walked over to the French door refrigerator, and took out the covered bowl of sliced cantaloupe and honeydew melon.

Reed put on the tea kettle, then poured six scoops of Lavazza Qualitia Rossa coffee into a French press carafe.

"You're not going to grind some whole beans?" Ravel interjected.

Reed exhaled.

"No, not with my husband still sleeping."

"*My husband ... my husband ... my husband,*" Ravel whined under her breath.

She was terribly in love with Reed, yet Reed did not return the love. She was too committed, too enthralled, too much in love with one Jacob Dupree.

The whistling tea kettle prompted Reed to pour boiling water on top of the fresh coffee grounds in the French press.

"In four minutes, we plunge, ladies."

"The Lavazza smells so good," Chenoa said. "And, Reed, I'm sorry for ambushing you today. Ravel can be very persuasive sometimes."

"Yes, yes she can. But no worries, Chenoa. I'm very protective of my Swiss genius. She acts all tough and independent, yet I know for a fact she doesn't mind my having her back."

Ravel had just stuffed a miniature cream puff *and* dainty eclair in her mouth.

When she said, "Pfft!" to Reed's remark, pastry flakes flew out of her mouth.

Reed chuckled as she poured freshly brewed Italian coffee into three diner style coffee mugs.

"We bought these mugs from a hipster coffee shop in San Francisco called Subterranean Brews."

"I like 'em" Ravel said. "Ever notice how coffee tastes better in a white china coffee mug?"

Chenoa sipped her coffee.

"You know, I think you're right, Ravel."

Ravel smooched a kiss to Chenoa.

Chenoa gave her a demure wink.

Good to see the mongoose and the cobra getting along, Reed thought.

She took a bite of a mousse cream pie.

"So good. Hmm, I guess I better turn on my phone. Sure was nice being off the grid for a little while."

Reed checked for recent calls and messages.

"Look at that, Andre called me four times this morning."

Andre had left a voicemail.

Reed tapped play.

The message was brief and horrific: "Reed, my God, please call me. Someone kidnapped my baby brother."

10

―――――

It was eight a.m. on Monday in downtown Tampa.

Traffic was heavy and the sidewalks crowded—never a good combination, since Florida drivers viewed pedestrians as little more than annoying speed bumps.

Tampa City Hall and the Hillsborough County Center were alive with activity.

Litigators, shrouded in black suits, pulled large trial cases on wheels as they marched confidently into the federal and state courthouses.

A great flock of field-tripping middle schoolers set upon the historic Tampa Theatre to view a special screening of Alfred Hitchcock's *The Birds*.

A bellicose street preacher, wearing aviator sunglasses, a railroad-striped seersucker suit, and Tar Heel blue Air Jordans, stood on Franklin Street and launched into a diatribe against the LGBTQ+ community.

"God created real rainbows, not queer rainbows," he shouted into a bullhorn.

A teacher accompanying the middle schoolers heard the street preacher's bigotry. She stopped walking and said to the preacher, "You, sir, are a complete cretin."

Her students cheered and clapped.

The preacher scoffed and dismissively waved off his detractors, hoping to shock and awe other bystanders over to his way of thinking.

And on the top floor of a commercial skyscraper, Reed O'Hara sat at her ultra-modern Kennedy executive desk in her law office. Even though the office space came at a premium, Reed thought it was worth it for the view alone.

Plus, she'd developed a kind of kinship with the kettle of turkey vultures riding thermals around her building. She admired the birds' broad wingspan, two-tone brown plumage, featherless red heads, and pale beaks. She learned the raptors soared at extreme heights to gain a better vantage point on their prey.

Pretty much what I do sometimes, she thought.

Reed was conducting a strategy session focused on locating Vlad, Andre's kidnapped brother.

Joining her were Andre, Jake, Ravel, and Chenoa, along with Hillsborough County Homicide Detective Pete Langdon. Since Andre reported the kidnapping to the Tampa Police Department, the case was technically out of Detective Langdon's jurisdiction. However, he was eager to participate in this meeting, as he and Reed had developed a professional comradeship.

"Pete, thanks so much for coming here today," Reed said. "I know we'll all benefit from your vast experience in law enforcement."

Langdon sat in one of five chairs fronting Reed's desk. He wore a XXL Tampa Bay Buccaneers tee shirt, loose-fitting jeans, and black Sketcher's slip-on sneakers. His Smith & Wesson .38 Special was holstered on his belt and covered over by the Bucs shirt.

"Happy to help out, Reed. I only hope this kidnapping doesn't turn into a homicide, even though that'd be more in my wheelhouse."

With his hands clasped in front of him, Andre lowered his head and exhaled loudly.

"Oh, sorry, Andre, it's hard sometimes to be diplomatic in my line of work," Langdon said. "But really, my man, you want me to give it to you straight, not just hold your Sasquatch-sized hand."

At times, Detective Langdon could be a difficult person to handle.

Two years ago, he was part of a task force tracking an assassin who targeted Catholic priests in Tampa Bay—pedophilic retired Catholic priests, to be more exact. Reed also was searching for this killer, as the Vatican's Father Angel hired her for a more discreet investigation. It was inevitable Detective Langdon and Reed crossed paths, then swords.

The first meeting went wrong from the start. Langdon wouldn't stop ogling Reed, even letting slip a crude remark about her breasts. Fortunately, Reed buried the hatchet with the detective. Admittedly, her first thought was to bury the hatchet *in* Langdon. Both Reed and Langdon were instrumental in capturing the assassins. Reed preferred to keep a low profile afterwards, though Detective Langdon received commendations for closing the case of the pervy priest killers. And just like Rick Blaine and Captain Louis Renault at the end of *Casablanca*, it was the start of a beautiful friendship between Reed and Langdon, so long as he kept his prurient thoughts to himself.

"I get what you're saying, Detective," Andre said. "I just can't think about Vlad dying."

Langdon slapped the arm of his chair.

"Well, you better buckle up, buttercup. All of you in this room best be prepared for the worst outcome here. These skels looked like they knew what they were doing. *Somebody* got them good and ready for that rapid-fire takedown."

Everyone waited for Reed to respond.

She cleared her throat.

"I get your point, Pete. Care to hazard a guess as to why they grabbed Vlad?"

Langdon pondered Reed's question.

"No ransom demand yet?"

"No," Andre said.

"That's odd—ransom demands usually come within twenty-four hours of the kidnapping."

"Was it a mistake for me to report it to the police?"

"Not at all, Andre. The more people looking for Vlad, the better odds we'll find him. But you know what, I can't get my head wrapped around as to why your brother was taken."

Jake leaned forward slightly in his chair.

"It doesn't make sense, Pete. Vlad leads a righteous life, he stays out of trouble, doesn't use drugs, makes a comfortable living, no apparent reason at all for his kidnapping."

Langdon flicked his front teeth with a thumbnail, making a pronounced clicking sound.

That's so annoying, but maybe it helps the guy think, Chenoa thought.

Today, Chenoa wore a burgundy Halston silk dress with cognac Prada boots, one of her more understated outfits. Having forsaken her vows as a Catholic nun and leaving the Church entirely, she felt completely free to try out any fashion that caught her eye. But it was a very expensive awakening—the Prada boots alone cost her three thousand dollars. She felt no compunction, however, depleting her bank account in order to fill her wardrobe with classic and cutting-edge haute couture.

Though Chenoa sat as far from Detective Langdon as possible, he still eyed her. Having transformed into a gorgeous woman, she struggled with the attention she received from men.

Oh, Momma, that's one gorgeous ginger, Langdon thought.

"Andre, you're sure these white guys had on black face?" he asked.

"Yes, I am, Detective."

"Hmm, maybe the ringleader is having a little fun here, you know, cracking wise about Black-on-Black crime."

Jake looked at Reed, who nodded yes to him.

"What?" Langdon asked them.

"Pete, what if Vlad were not the intended target?" Reed asked.

"Hmm, very interesting. I mean, the entire takedown seemed so premeditated, you know, well planned out, precise. Don't make sense this team would jack the first Black guy they see."

"Too arbitrary, right?" Jake said.

Chenoa interjected: "Try this on for size, Detective,"

Like to try you on...no, stop it, dirtbag, Langdon thought.

"Let's hear it, young lady."

"Okay, it's implausible this was a gang of racists trolling Tampa Bay for just any Black person to kidnap. I think they had a very specific mission. Think about it, y'all, who does Vlad closely resemble? What if this were a case of mistaken identity?"

"What?" Andre gasped.

"Yes, my friend, I hate to say this, but I suspect you were the intended target," Chenoa said.

"Oh, no, why, why would they come after me?"

Ravel didn't look up from her laptop when she said, "You're a major piece in this chess game, Andre. I'd say you're the black knight. But you're not the king, and that's who these creeps are after."

Reed smiled warmly at Ravel.

"Thanks for taking yourself off mute," Reed said sans sarcasm.

Ravel returned the smile.

"For you, anything ... King Reed."

This time, Langdon slapped his knee.

"Ha! I think Ravel and the redhead are right! Good job, ladies."

Chenoa looked straight into Langdon's beady brown eyes.

"My name is Chenoa, Detective."

"Pleased to meet you, Chenoa. You and Ravel make a good team, you know that?"

"Yes, when we are not insulting one another."

Ravel threw her hands in the air.

"Jumpin' Jack Flash, I'm the brains of this outfit. Chenoa is merely my wingman."

"Your wingman? Really? Why don't you just ...."

Reed clapped her hands sharply.

"Chenoa, Ravel, that's enough. Right now. Your unprofessional behavior won't be tolerated. Please stop embarrassing yourselves."

There was complete silence for twenty seconds.

"I apologize for my lack of professionalism, Reed, it won't happen again," Chenoa said.

Ravel continued to stare at her laptop screen.

"Yeah, what she said."

"Very well," Reed said. "Now I think you two are on to something here."

"I agree, so let's fine tune this theory," Jake said. "Let's assume

Andre was the target of this kidnapping. I think Ravel's right, abducting Andre gets him out of the way."

"Are you suggesting, Jake, that you and I are the real targets here?" Reed said.

"Yes, ma'am, I am."

"Think about it, folks," Chenoa said, gaining more confidence by the minute. "Get Andre out of the way and Reed becomes more vulnerable—sorry, Jake, no offense intended, but Reed is the intended target."

Jake waved his right hand.

"No offense taken, Chenoa. I have my share of people who'd like to get back at me, but this is about Reed and Namaste. What really concerns me is this person seems too bright to be so obvious."

Reed tapped her Mont Blanc pen.

Kinda scary how much we think alike, she thought.

"Jake, it's because she wants to be obvious, she wants me to know she's coming for me."

Jake exhaled.

He'd almost lost Reed when she was shot in the course of tracking down Don Coyote. Fortunately, she wore a Kevlar vest. Now it appeared someone else wanted to harm her, and Jake simply couldn't lose Reed, the center of his universe.

"She's a cocky son of a gun, Reed. I agree, she's conspiring in plain sight."

Ravel tsked loudly.

"There you two go again, Reed, operating in the Cone of Silence. Who are you talking about?"

"I'm talking about a pit bull disguised as a Yorkshire terrier. An extremely dangerous pit bull, in this case. I am talking about a white racist menace named Raven Doyle."

11

———

"Talk about the ghost of Poe rearing its big old head," Ravel said.

Langdon nodded in agreement.

I'll just pretend I know what the heck she is talking about, he said to himself.

"Who's this Raven Doyle?" Langdon asked.

"We met her and her husband Chance at the Hangar on New Year's Eve," Reed said.

Langdon did a double take.

"Hold on there, you mean to tell me you and Jake actually went out on New Year's?"

Reed gave him a three-star-out-of-a-possible-five Mona Lisa smile.

"Yes, Peter, we sometimes have a life beyond our work."

Never good when she calls me "Peter", he thought.

"Yes, ma'am, I know you do, I was being a wisenheimer. So tell me about Raven and Chance Doyle."

Reed laid down her Mont Blanc pen and folded her hands on the desk.

"Raven owns a horse farm in northwest Hillsborough County...."

"Sorry, but does Chance own the horse farm as well?" Langdon interjected.

"I don't know," Reed replied.

"No, he does not—her family has owned the farm since 1853, she's the sole owner of four-hundred acres of primo real estate," Ravel said casually, not looking up from her laptop.

"How do you know that?" Langdon asked with an incredulous tone in his voice.

Ravel laughed.

"Everything, and I mean everything, is on the internets."

Let her riff, she'll get there all in good time, Reed mused.

She has the patience of a saint, Ravel thought.

"It's a matter of having the brains and the know-how to find private information. Forgive me for my immodesty, Columbo, but I'm a good hacker."

"Best in the world, in my humble opinion," Reed said.

Ravel batted her long eyelashes at Reed.

"Perhaps I am, but there are dozens of hackers out in the digital ether trying to de-throne me."

Langdon spoke up.

"So we can agree Raven Doyle owns a horse farm on a very expensive piece of land in one of the more upper-class areas in the county. How does that make her a suspect?"

Jake sat up in his chair.

"It doesn't, Pete. Yet on Saturday night, Raven went out of her way to convince us she was a white supremacist."

"Was she recruiting you?"

"Not at all," Reed said. "It was more like she was setting up the pieces on a chessboard. She made it clear she and I were polar opposites as to racial issues."

"One more thing, Pete," Jake said.

"What's that?"

"Reed and I talked about Raven when we got home from the Hangar."

Ravel's eyes twinkled.

"You mean just before you did the nasty?"

"Ravel!" Reed said.

"Sorry, couldn't resist."

Looks like Ravel gets in more trouble with Reed than I do, Langdon thought.

"You two had a chit-chat about this woman. What did you figure out?"

"Reed and I sensed Raven reconnoitered us before our encounter at the Hangar. I think she's well aware Reed is as pro-active with people of color as she is with women."

Langford looked at Ravel.

"Could Raven Doyle get all of this about Reed off the *internets?*"

Ravel giggled.

"Of course, Inspector Clouseau. Even a monkey without a 'lee-sance' could do it."

Langford laughed loudly.

"Yeah, yeah, I get it with the Pink Panther references. You're a real wise guy, and I like it."

"Excellent, knowing that will help me sleep better tonight."

Ravel stole a glance over at Andre.

"Please don't think we are not taking this situation seriously enough, my dear Andre."

Ravel and Andre were the very best of friends. It was merely a matter of one outsider finding the other. Andre loved Ravel in the purest sense of the word. He was almost as protective of her as he was of Reed.

"No, Ravel, I wasn't thinking that at all. We are a band of professionals and this is our process—the quips and jabs and teasing make us think harder. And I believe I understand this whole situation so much better: Raven Doyle wants to destroy Reed and Namaste, and to do that, she needs to cripple our defenses, which is why those Dixie donut holes mistakenly grabbed Vlad—they wanted to eliminate me."

"You mean kidnap you," Chenoa said.

Andre shook his head no. His large brown eyes filled with tears.

Detective Langdon put his hand on Andre's forearm.

"Let me have this, Andre," Langdon said. "Unfortunately, Chenoa, that wasn't a kidnapping, in retrospect. Remember, no ransom demand, not word one from these creeps. They don't intend on giving back Vlad, especially when they figure out, or at least Raven Doyle figures out, the wrong guy got jacked."

Chenoa rose from her chair, walked over to Andre, held his face with both hands, and kissed him lightly on the forehand.

Well, well, well, Langdon thought.

"Andre, I am so sorry for Vlad and for you," Chenoa said in a soothing voice. "We must move as quickly as possible to get him back safe and sound."

Andre smiled almost lovingly at Chenoa and held her delicate hand. "Thank you, Chenoa," he whispered.

Reed was about to speak when her office manager Roman Delaney slowly opened the office door.

"Reed, I am so sorry to interrupt, but Augustus Wagram insists on speaking with you."

Reed appeared annoyed.

"For heaven's sake, why?"

"It's about Megan, she's missing."

12

"If I may speak on behalf of the cheap seats here, just who is this Megan?" Langdon asked. "And who's Augustus Ingram? Geesh, before you know it, Porfiry Petrovich will come waltzing in."

Ravel golf clapped Langdon.

"Well, done, Detective, who would of thunk you read *Crime and Punishment*."

Langdon acknowledged Ravel's sideways compliment with a regal wave.

"Whatever, Ravioli, and I bet Swiss francs to biscotti that you aren't aware Columbo was based on Petrovich."

Ravel squinted at him.

"Go ahead, Wangfurt, call me 'Ravioli' again."

"Or what, young lady?"

"I'll clean out your pension and donate the money to Planned Parenthood."

Ravel knew Langdon was a devout Catholic; donating his pension funds to Planned Parenthood couldn't be more devastating.

"You wouldn't dare."

"Oh, I most certainly would," Ravel said. "But, hey, I'll concede you figured out I'm Swiss, though I'm French Swiss, not Italian, Detective Wang Chung."

Before Langdon could respond, Reed stepped in.

"All right, all right, that's enough, both of you," she said. "And Pete, Megan is head bartender at the Hangar's Flight Lounge. She and Raven got cozy with one another on New Year's Eve."

"Ok, so what about Augustus Ingram?"

Ravel laughed a bit too loudly.

Reed shot blue-eyed darts at her.

"It's Wagram, Augustus Wagram. He is the Hangar's GM and a father figure to Megan, so we should take seriously his concern for her."

"Roger that," Langdon said.

Roman remained silent as he stood in the doorway.

"Roman, show Augustus in, please," Reed said.

"Yes, ma'am."

With a crook handle Malacca walking stick balanced on his left forearm, Augustus marched into Reed's office and didn't stop until he reached the left side of her desk.

He wore a black Ralph Lauren suit with a pink dress shirt and a purple silk tie with a matching pocket square. He completed his outfit with burgundy Chelsea boots.

Those ankle boots are definitely Beckett Simonon, Chenoa thought. Man, oh Manischewitz, and people think I'm a clothes hound.

Augie baby is the epitome of antiquiche cool, Ravel said to herself.

"Mrs. O'Hara, thank you so much for allowing me an audience with you, and I'm most apologetic for not calling first."

"Augustus, please call me Reed. I understand from Roman you are worried about Megan."

"I am *terribly* worried about Megan, Reed. We have an agreement in place: she is to call me each night when she arrives home from work. That way, I know she's safe and I can sleep peacefully. Megan has kept to this arrangement for over two years. Until last Saturday night—New Year's Eve, of course."

"She didn't call at all?" Reed asked.

"No, she did not. At around six a.m., I started calling her. No answer. I left multiple messages. No response. I went to her apartment in Brandon. No one came to the door. Her lovely red Fiat Spider wasn't in its reserved parking space. It's as if she has vanished."

Reed listened sympathetically to Augustus.

"Perhaps she met up with someone and stayed the night with her."

Augustus smiled slightly.

"You are both kind and sensitive, Reed. You always have been with regards to our community. However, Megan calls me if she stays over at someone else's home. Of that, I am most certain. No, something awful has happened to my sweet Megan. I can sense it."

Reed rose from her desk, walked over to Augustus, and held his right hand.

Goodness, his hand is so soft, and check out that manicure—I'm jelly, she thought.

"Augustus, we will do everything in our power to find Megan. In fact, I already have an idea where she is."

His eyes widened like Marty Feldman's in *Young Frankenstein*.

"Where is she, please tell me, *please*."

Reed put her arm under Augustus' and gently walked him to the open doorway.

"Please try to be patient, my friend. It's only a hunch, which we'll check out as soon as possible."

Roman stood patiently in the front office. He was an HIV-positive gay man who had attended several Rainbow Pride events with both Megan and Augustus.

In the parlance of Bill Clinton, Roman felt the elderly man's pain.

"Augustus, I'm putting Roman in charge of staying in touch with you," Reed said. "Should we find Megan, we'll contact you immediately."

A tear rolled down his cheek as Augustus took Reed's hand and kissed it ever so lightly.

"Truly, Reed O'Hara, you are a scholar and a gentlewoman. Thank you so very much."

Augustus joined Roman in the front office.

Reed closed the office door and returned to her desk.

"You know, y'all, we don't purposefully make things complicated—that's the way they get by all by their lonesome."

Ravel gave Reed a thumbs up, then said, "True that, fearless leader."

Langdon harrumphed good-naturedly.

"I don't suppose, fearless leader, you have a plan yet, not that I'm rushing you or anything," the detective asked.

Ravel winked her approval at Langdon.

Talk about the most unlikely of bromances, Reed said to herself.

Reed began tapping her pen on the desk.

Those wheels are turning, just let her be, Jake thought.

Note to self, have Roman validate my parking, Langdon reminded himself.

Black suit, pink dress shirt, purple tie—Augustus is divine, simply divine, Chenoa thought.

Gotta admit that Augustus is a charming geezer, Ravel allowed to herself.

Bet that Raven Doyle has both Vlad and Megan, what a monster, Andre thought.

"Are we ready?" Reed asked.

Everyone nodded yes.

"Andre, you are to protect Namaste full-time—Raven may have something in the works for our nightclub. Let no harm come to our performers and staff."

Andre didn't hesitate to respond: "Yes, ma'am, received and understood."

"Good. Jake, divide your time between coordinating searches for Vlad and helping Andre keep Namaste secure. I'll join you in the search for Vlad when I can."

"You got it, Reed," Jake said with confidence.

"Excellent. Ravel and Chenoa, you're tasked with finding Megan. I'm confident Raven has control of her. Get the word out in your networks. We find Megan, we could find Vlad, too. I might have a devious little plan that could involve Sehar, okay?"

"Look at your bad self," Ravel said. "Raven has a horse farm, and our tiny Sehar can ride like a demon."

Reed raised her eyebrows and smiled.

"Pete, thanks for your input today. As usual, you were brilliant and mostly well-behaved."

"Aw, shucks, Reed," Langdon said.

"May we call on you if we need you in a more official capacity?"

"You bet, call anytime, good buddy."

Reed stood and put both hands on her desk.

"Let's do this, folks."

13

Brunch time at the Jackson Equestrian Estate in northwest Hillsborough County.

Raven and Chance were outside on the brick patio of their mansion. The couple sat in white wrought-iron chairs at a white wrought-iron table shaded by a red heart-shaped patio umbrella. Azalea bushes bordering the brick patio showed off early season purple blooms. Being high noon, the bright Florida sun lit up the nearby pastures of perfect Kentucky bluegrass. The true-blue sky signaled low humidity. A comfortable breeze generated a red dust devil on the training track. Over in the far pasture, a string of thoroughbreds raced about as if they were wild mustangs. Only the sound of banging hammers coming from behind a stable marred this idyllic scene.

Raven held a large Bloody Mary ruddered by a skewer of blackened shrimp, fresh cherry tomatoes, maple bacon, and langostino tails. She bit into a shrimp with the ferocity of a hangry piranha then drank a good four fingers of her Bloody Mary.

"Ever tell you how my great-great-grandfather Jackson caused an Indian war over by the Caloosahatchee River around 1848?"

Chance poured himself more Folgers coffee from an antique sterling silver coffee pot.

"Don't recollect that story about John Jackson."

He drank his coffee black, as he believed cream and sugar were for the limp-wristed crowd.

"Yeah, it was before he bought all this land to raise cattle and horses."

"He actually started an Indian war?"

Raven held her skewer as if it were a royal scepter and her highball glass a globus cruciger.

She polished off her Bloody Mary then belched like a boilermaker.

"That's my girl," Chance said approvingly.

Raven wiped her mouth with the back of her hand.

"To be honest, it was more of a skirmish. A few whites died, and a whole mess of Indians got sent to their happy hunting grounds."

"And your great-grandfather caused this? How?"

"Well, what happened was, Old Grand-Dad was a land surveyor at the time. He was supposed to survey land held by white settlers. And, oopsie! He wandered over to Indian land and started surveying. Indians didn't like it at all. Not one bit. So the killing started. On both sides. Luckily, Old Grand-Dad vamoosed before the Indians could get him. Federal troops had to come in and pacify, shall we say, said restless natives. True story."

Chance worked on a bagel topped with cream cheese, lox, capers, and red onion while he listened to Raven's story.

"You got cream cheese in your mustache, buddy," Raven said. "Why do you eat that crap? What's wrong with a Boston cream donut?"

Chance let the cream cheese stay in his mustache, knowing it annoyed Raven.

"Bagel too ethnic for you, Rave?"

"Absolutely."

She couldn't stand it any longer: she smooshed the cream cheese out of Chance's mustache.

"Thank you, ma'am. You're a good wife, you know. And I liked your story about OG. Never underestimate the power of an altazimuth theodolite to stir up trouble with the redskins."

Chance gave Raven a smile whiskered with smugness.

Raven smiled back at him.

"A regular old surveyor's sextant would just be effective in mapping out an Indian land grab."

Chance leaned across the table and kissed his wife.

"Brilliant, beautiful, and devious—what more could a man ask for."

Raven giggled lasciviously.

"Don't forget the occasional threesome, my love."

Chance sat back in his chair.

"Speaking of which," he said sullenly.

"Don't you worry, Megan is coming along just fine. She has all the makings of a perfect sub. Just needs a little more seasoning, then you can join us. Remember, you gorgeous hunk of a man, the pleasure isn't so much in doing the thing, the true pleasure is in planning it."

"What are we talking about here, Megan or Reed O'Hara?"

"Ha! You goose, Reed is my number one project, Megan is more of a naughty hobby. Let's not get vocation and avocation mixed up, all right?"

"Yes, ma'am. Something tells me you've got something in mind for this week, you know, before we go over to that nightclub on Friday."

Raven popped a large cherry tomato into her mouth. When she bit down on the tomato, its juice squirted out of her mouth and dribbled down her chin.

Chance used a gray cloth napkin to wipe her mouth and chin.

"Thank you, kind sir. And yuppers, I got a little sumpin' sumpin' planned for Namaste, probably Wednesday."

"Good, I'm about done with my assignment. Needs a little fine tuning, is all."

Raven patted his knee.

"Don't rush it, Chance. You still have plenty of time. I know I can count on you for quality work."

"Rah, baby."

"You really are my cute little jarhead."

The hammering behind the stable finally stopped.

"Let's go over and see how Colt and Megan are doing with their project," Chance said.

"All right, but we have to be sure everything's in place for tonight's festivities."

"No worries, love. It's all gonna come together just fine and dandy."
Raven and Chance held hands as they strolled over to the stable.

14

Raven and Chance walked through the stable, which was pristine clean, meticulously organized, and well-appointed for the racing thoroughbreds.

They found Colt and Megan taking a break outside of the stable.

Colt was smoking a cigarette.

Megan drank water from a large Tervis Tumbler bearing the Albert Einstein Gator logo of the University of Florida.

Without saying a word, Raven took the plastic cup out of Megan's hand and splashed the water on Colt and his lit cigarette.

"Boy, how many times have I told you not to smoke anywhere on my land, especially near the stable?"

Colt was twenty-two years old, tall and gangly, high school educated, and a former meth addict.

Raven met him at a horse show at the Florida State Fairgrounds. She got him off meth, then took him on as a ranch hand.

Though she had a soft spot for the young man, Raven vehemently protected her horses.

"Ma'am, I am so sorry."

Raven tsked disdainfully.

"I've a good mind to send you down the road ... or even worse."

Colt knew what Raven was threatening; he had, in fact, participated in the disposal of individuals who incurred Raven's wrath.

"Miss Raven, you are the light of my life. You have healed me and helped me to see the power of a white race unified. I promise not to disappoint you again."

What a steaming pile of blarney blather, Megan said to herself.

Colt saw Megan staring at him.

Whatever woman, my life's on the line here, he thought.

"This is your last mulligan, boy," Raven said. "And I mean your absolute last, do you feel me?"

"Yes, ma'am. I understand, and thank you."

Chance walked by Colt and shook his head in disgust at him.

"You have no idea, young Colt, no idea at all."

"I think I do, sir."

"Well good. So let's take a look-see at your work."

A large oak cross lay on the ground. It was a good eight-feet tall and an easy six-feet wide.

"Megan and I were wondering if y'all want us to varnish it."

Chance smiled devilishly.

"Nope. This ain't a burning cross, boy. More like a crucifixion cross, isn't that right, Mrs. Doyle?"

Raven simply smiled at Chance.

Turning into a lovely day, she thought.

"And sir, we used dowel joints, just like you ordered. There are twelve dowel joints, six on each side of the cross beam. You're absolutely right, sir, dowel joints are a whole lot better than pocket holes."

"Yeah, well, I have more than a little experience with constructing wooden crosses," Chance said.

He winked at Raven, who winked back.

"Can I say something about Megan, Mr. and Mrs. Doyle?" Colt asked.

Raven nodded yes.

"I wasn't too sure Megan was gonna be much help, her being a girl and all. Well sure enough, you shoulda seen how she handled that doweling jig. Like a professional, she was."

Raven smiled warmly at Megan.

"Look at my Irish beauty—slings drinks with panache, handy with carpentry tools, sharp as a braided leather flogger."

Megan's face blushed bright red.

"I'm honored to help out in any way I can, Raven."

"How sturdy is that cross, Megan?" Chance asked.

Megan looked down and kicked dirt with her sneaker.

"It'll hold at least three-hundred pounds, no problem at all," she said confidently.

"Where'd you pick up your carpenter skills?" Chance asked.

Megan got shy all of a sudden.

"Don't really like bragging on myself, Chance, but I'm something of an autodidact. Taught myself how to tend bar. Whenever there was a brawl at a pub, and there was damaged furniture and such, I figured out how to fix a busted chair or an off-kilter table."

Chance clapped.

"Very good, Megan. You've become a nice asset around here in a real short time."

Megan beamed, "Like I said, I'll help any way I can."

Chance gave her his diamond melting smile.

"I'll remember that, young lady."

Raven stepped forward.

"All right, enough of the flirting, you two."

Chance nodded yes.

"Yes, ma'am," Megan said quickly.

"Colt and Megan, y'all did a fine job with the cross, so I'm going to reward you," Raven said. "Colt, you get to see another sunrise; Megan, we're going to get you some genuine cowboy boots—those sneakers are really annoying."

"Thank you, Raven, I've never owned cowboy boots," Megan said.

Colt wisely stayed silent, realizing that his reward was a life saver. Think I'd best get some of that nicotine gum, he thought.

Strutting like the cock of the walk, Jimmie ambled up to the group. He was a veteran ranch hand. A short towhead, he looked much younger than his actual age of thirty-two. He was trying to grow a beard, but his face was a patchwork of tumbleweed whiskers. During a summit meeting of the Sons of the Confederacy and the Ku Klux

Klan, Chance encountered Jimmie. Chance liked the younger man's confidence, his vicious hatred of Black and brown people, and the fact that Jimmie already had three kills notched in his western belt buckle.

"Mr. and Mrs. Doyle, I bet y'all are pumped about tonight," Jimmie said.

He popped a piece of nicotine gum in his mouth, making sure Raven and Chance saw him do it.

Won't be long, Colt good buddy, afore I'm spreading your body parts all over the woods, Jimmie thought.

"Yes, Jimmie, we're excited," Raven said. "I need to give you and Colt very specific instructions. No room for error, all right?"

"Can't speak for Colt, but I sure won't let you down, ma'am."

You little dung beetle, Colt thought.

"Don't need Jimmie boy to speak for me, ma'am. I'll follow your instructions to the T guaranteed."

"What is most important, my boys, is that you have our guest on the cross and in full display at ten p.m.," Raven said with conviction. "Have the cross planted fifty feet from the veranda no later than six p.m. Got it?"

Both Colt and Jimmie said "Yes, ma'am" at the same time.

"Now—and listen up here. Set-up two spotlights, but don't turn them on, Chance'll signal when it's time."

Chance simply said, "Rah, baby."

She smiled lovingly at her husband.

Sure enough picked me a peach, she thought.

"One last thing," Raven said.

She reached out and held Megan's hand.

"Bring Megan along and let her tie up our guest, okay?"

Again, Colt and Jimmie simultaneously said, "Yes, ma'am".

Megan hugged Raven.

"I'm speechless, Raven, thank you so much,"

Raven kissed her on the cheek.

"You'd better believe it, hon. I want you to be part of a glorious night. Besides, I've already noticed you know your way around knots. You were very helpful the other night teaching me different types of restriction knots."

Megan blushed the color of Jake's Mr. Lincoln roses.

"Raven, what do you say we go and pay a visit to our guest of honor," Chance suggested.

Raven giggled.

"Good idea, I haven't seen him yet."

Yes indeed, this is how you bring in a new year, she declared to herself.

Led by Raven, the group walked in the direction of the horse farm's woodshed.

15

Like most everything else on the Jackson Equestrian Estate, the woodshed was as attractive as it was utilitarian. The twelve-foot by twelve-foot shed was an exact replica of a ranch house, right down to its red cedar exterior, treated pine shingle roof, two front windows, a covered porch with railings, and two hitching posts. Raven insisted pots of red and white impatiens be placed below each window. One halfway expected diminutive wranglers bunked inside, perhaps playing cards at a tiny poker table.

"Got this idea from the Swiss and their postcard-pretty alpine barns in the mountain pastures," Raven said. "Hardly anyone knows some of those barns house artillery in case of an invasion. Called hiding in plain sight."

And today, the woodshed held captive a kidnapped Black man hidden in plain sight. An antique iron lock secured the front door. The windows were covered from the inside with blackout curtains.

Jimmie, aided by the teenaged Burris and a middle-aged ranch hand named Lester, cleared out the various tools from the woodshed before depositing the kidnapped man in it.

"Place is almost too nice for him, ma'am," Jimmie said.

"Have to agree with you on that one." Raven replied. "Did he put up much of a fight once you got him here?"

"Naw, he was just a big old puddy tat, he was."

Chance immediately slapped the back of Jimmie's head. It was a hard slap coming from a big man, so Jimmie stumbled forward and dropped to his knees.

"Why'd you do that, sir?"

"You never say 'Naw' to Raven Doyle. You shoulda said, 'No, ma'am'."

Um huh, and so it starts, Colt thought.

Jimmie's time on this earth may have gotten shorter, Megan said to herself.

She helped him get on his feet while whispering to him, "Apologize, you moron."

"Mr. and Mrs. Doyle, I am sorry for my rudeness. I really mean it, I am sorry."

Raven stepped in front of him, gently guiding Megan away from him with her small right hand.

"Your problem, boy, is you're getting way too familiar with your boss," Raven said. "Plus, I saw you eyeballing Megan. You'd better wise up, like real fast. Grace Baptist Church! Why am I having trouble today with my two favorite boys?"

Megan reached over and held Raven's hand.

We got ourselves a risk taker, Chance thought.

"Raven, it's going to be okay, boys will be boys, as in complete oafs and idiots. They can't help themselves," Megan said. "But you know what, we still need them."

Raven placed Megan's hand over her heart.

"You're right, sweetie. My, oh my, I may keep you around just to keep me out of the swamp sulks."

Megan kept her hand resting on Raven's chest. Has the heartbeat of a Bengal tiger, she thought.

"You're one special lady, Raven, I will serve you in any capacity."

Raven silently congratulated herself for how quickly she had converted Megan.

"All right, let's take a gander at this creature," she said.

Jimmie practically ran to the front door to unlock the shed.

He opened the door and held it for Raven.

Smart lad, Megan thought.

Raven peered inside before entering. She barely made out a large Black man sitting on the plywood floor. He wore a slave collar lock that was chained to a support beam. He also had his wrists and ankles in wrought-iron shackles.

"Ma'am, those are genuine slave shackles," Jimmie said proudly. "We stole them from that Old Slave Mart up in Charleston."

He handed Raven a lit flashlight.

"That's a police baton flashlight, ma'am—if'n you had to, you could split his Black coconut head right easy—ma'am."

Chance winked his approval to Jimmie, who blushed slightly.

"Well, then, let's take a look," Raven said eagerly.

Standing in the doorway, she focused the flashlight beam on the chained Black man.

Vlad looked at her defiantly.

"To whom can I complain about these primitive lodgings?" he asked.

Raven dropped the flashlight.

"No, no, no. It can't be. It just can't be. How could this of happened? Sweet Jesus, why have You abandoned me?"

She cried and whimpered uncontrollably.

Chance came up behind Raven and put his giant hands on her small shoulders.

"Rave, what's wrong? Talk to me."

Raven simply pointed to Vlad.

Though the flashlight was on the floor and its beam askew, Chance still saw it was Vlad, not Andre, in chains.

"What a first-class screw up," he said. "How on earth did we get the wrong guy?"

Raven spun around as quickly as a Florida racer snake.

"You were in charge, Jimmie. Explain yourself. Right now, you know, if you don't mind."

She had stopped ugly crying, though her cheeks remained wet with tears and a small dribble of snot rolled over her lips.

Jimmie was near speechless.

"What, this flabbergasts me, ma'am, I don't get it."

Raven slapped him.

"If you say one word about all darkies looking alike, I will nail you to that cross over there and set it on fire."

"Ma'am, please, yeah, I was in charge, but I asked Colt if that was Andre, and he said yes."

Colt stomped the ground with his cowboy boot.

"That's a bold-face lie, Jimmie, you never asked me nothing about nothing. You were your usual big man running the show. I tried to tell you we should be real certain, but no, you ignored me."

Jimmie shot back, "Talk about a bold-face lie."

Raven chopped her right hand into the palm of her left hand.

"Enough, no more, both of you boneheads. The reality of the sit-u-ation is we have Vlad as our floor show tonight."

"Sure am sorry, ma'am," Jimmie said.

Raven smiled at him. "Spilt milk under the bridge, hon," she said in a maternal tone.

Don't do it, Jimmie, she's baiting you, Megan thought.

"Ma'am, don't you mean *water* under the bridge?"

Chance waited for the explosion. One Mississippi, two Mississippi, three Mississippi, he counted to himself.

Raven kicked Jimmie between the legs, rammed her knee into his stomach, then right hooked him in the face, most certainly breaking his nose.

For the second time that day, Jimmie collapsed on the ground.

As Raven started after him, Chance grabbed her by the waist from behind and pulled her off the ground. "Breathe, hon. Hurt him anymore, we'll have to take him to the hospital. This ain't the time for answering questions from nosy Jew doctors."

Raven exhaled loudly. She appeared calm.

Man knows how to handle his wife and that wicked temper of hers, Megan thought.

"Sorry, I was all in my feels," Raven said. "Thanks for helping me to gain a wee bit of perspective."

Once again, Megan helped Jimmie off the ground.

She whispered to him, "Not another word."

He nodded as blood dribbled from his nostrils.

"Megan, take Colt and Jimmie and get the cross up sturdy like," Raven said with authority. "You're in charge, my sassy lassie, so don't take any lip off these lunkheads."

"Yes, ma'am, right away," Megan responded. "Okay, cowboys, no time for a hitch in your git along."

Got that one from Andy Griffith, she recalled to herself.

Megan walked away in the direction of the stable; Colt and Jimmie, still holding his bloody nose, followed closely behind her.

Raven looked at Chance.

"Have to say, I need to control my temper better."

"Aw, heck, your temper is part of your charm.

Raven giggled like a teenager drinking her first bottle of Boone's Farm Strawberry Hill wine.

"Oh well, all great plans have their hiccups," she said. "We at least get Andre distracted big time, and folks tonight will have no idea about our screw up."

Chance gathered Raven into his arms.

"True that. Any last-minute instructions for me?"

Raven kissed Chance.

"Yes, sir, there is. I appreciate you want your way with Megan tonight after the festivities, and I don't have any problem with that. But please, before y'all hook up, do me a major solid."

Chance kissed her neck, then whispered in her ear, "Name it."

"Get rid of Jimmie. Have Colt help you."

"Rah, but how do you want me to get rid of him?"

An evil pall cast over Raven.

"Cut him into little tiny pieces and leave him for the coyotes."

"You don't want him buried?"

"Fine, bury his head, feet, and hands. There'll be plenty left over for the scavengers."

16

Later that same day, around seven p.m., the Jackson Equestrian Estate was ready for the evening's festivities.

A dozen Devonshire bronze lamp posts lined both sides of the estate's paved road, lighting the way for guests arriving at the antebellum mansion which resembled a kind of Deep South beacon, with its tall Corinthian columns and Byzantine dome lit by a cadre of spotlights. Like a gray calvary line, the guests streamed toward the mansion in Lincoln Navigators, Ford Mustangs, Cadillac Escalades, and Dodge Ram trucks. At any other gathering of white supremacists, the drivers would have blared their car horns to trumpet their arrival. However, out of respect for the Doyles' skittish thoroughbreds tucked away for the night in their stable, not one driver dared use his horn. A platoon of valets waited for the guests to pull into the circular driveway and dismount.

In less than an hour, over one-hundred guests had assembled on the large brick veranda behind the mansion.

Strings of white globe lights hoisted on poles bordered the veranda. Tiny fairy lights covered the hedge rows of blooming azalea bushes. There were two lighted flag poles in front of the stable. Unfurling in a gentle breeze were the Confederate flag and the United States flag. The Confederate flag was the same height as the Stars and Bars.

Exactly fifty feet from the veranda, the cross stood in darkness.

The guests milled about the two open bars.

The band Dixie Daze played old time bluegrass songs such as "Foggy Mountain Breakdown", "I Know You Rider", and "Orange Blossom Special". When Dixie Daze played "The Legend of the Rebel Soldier", a middle-aged woman holding a Jack and Coke highball swayed to the bluegrass music.

"That song makes me cry, it surely does," she said to no one in particular.

A man standing next to her wiped both of his eyes.

"Busts me up big time, Doris."

Doris and the crying man hugged.

His hand slid down her back and he patted her behind.

Doris pushed his hand away.

"Norville, stop that, not in front of people. You know better. Meet me over by the stable later on, you sex maniac."

Norville winked at Doris.

"You're my favorite Lady of the Invisible Empire, you know that, Doris darling?"

"Humph, I'd better be, Norv."

Doris' rotund husband didn't witness any of this illicit exchange, as he was too busy admiring the grand buffet—as usual, he was the first in line, waiting impatiently for the chuck wagon dinner bell to sound.

And truly, it was a feast of epicurean proportions. There were three roast suckling pigs, two rounds of beef, a deep-fried turkey, and several platters of Southern fried chicken. The sides were just as substantial: roasted corn on the cob, green beans simmered in lard and onions, fried okra, collard greens with ham hocks, grilled eggplant, Portobello mushroom caps stuffed with blue crab, Southern style potato salad, coleslaw with pineapple bits, and sweet cornbread. Desserts were showcased on a long table separated from the buffet. There were apple, cherry, pecan, and Georgia peach pies; old fashioned sour cream Bundt cakes; German chocolate cakes topped with coconut and pecan frosting; fudge brownies sprinkled with macadamia nuts; and strawberries from Plant City's first harvest topped with fresh whipped cream.

But everyone knew the dinner bell wouldn't sound until Raven Doyle made her grand entrance and addressed the crowd.

All of a sudden, Dixie Daze performed "Amazing Grace".

The crowd understood immediately that "Amazing Grace" was Raven's walk-up music.

An elderly Black butler opened the French doors leading out to the veranda. Their four black Labrador retrievers were quarantined inside the mansion.

Dressed in a white notched-collar poplin blouse, a gray kimono cardigan, black slacks, and deep red full-quill ostrich leather boots, Raven walked out with the confidence and gracefulness of a Milan runway model.

The crowd clapped and sang along with Dixie Daze.

Amazing Grace
How sweet the sound
That saved a wretch like me
I once was lost, but now I'm found
Was blind, but now I see

Chance urged the guests to gather around Raven.

He wore a collared shirt, jeans, cowboy boots, and a Stetson cowboy hat, all in black—he accomplished his sartorial goal of fading in the background.

"C'mon, y'all, keep singing this beautiful song!" Raven shouted.

My chains are gone
I've been set free
My God, my savior has ransomed me
And like a flood, His mercy rains

Little did these white supremacists know "Amazing Grace" was penned by the Englishman John Newton, a former captain of slave ships. Newton experienced a religious conversion and became an

Anglican clergyman. He was instrumental in England outlawing slavery in 1807. Raven, however, was aware of the song's history. A politician to her core, she never shared it with her followers.

What they don't know, won't get 'em confused and such, she thought. Besides, couldn't ask for a better intro song.

Chance helped Raven step up on a small plywood box painted black.

She purposefully scraped her boots on top of the black box.

"Just where we want 'em y'all, under our boot heel!"

The group cheered raucously.

"All right, settle it down, folks. You know, the coloreds had their so-called Emancipation Proclamation, though not one of us recognizes it, right?"

More loud cheering.

Even Doris' husband standing by the buffet hoo-hollered, though he steadfastly remained first in line.

"Tonight, I'm declaring *our* Dixie Emancipation Proclamation."

More applause and woo-hoos.

"We're not hiding any more. We are loud, proud, and endowed with mighty white rights. How many of y'all wear a Confederate flag trucker hat at the grocery store or the drug store nowadays and get a friendly nod, a knowing wink, even a handshake from fellow whites?"

Several people raised their hands.

"Good. Long as you're sure they ain't FBI or FDLE, talk with 'em, have a cup of coffee with 'em, bring 'em into the fold."

At least a dozen people answered, "Yes, ma'am!"

"Now, we are making real progress with placing our people on county commissions, school boards, county and state judges, as well as fourteen legislators doing God's work in Tallahassee. Heck, we have folks embedded in all sixty-seven county offices of election supervision. And law enforcement statewide is on our side. 'Fore long, Florida's going to go from being the Sunshine State to the Whiteshine State. Can I get an amen!"

This time, five or six men fired their pistols toward the starry sky.

People cheered both Raven and these men.

"Stop, gentlemen, you're going to upset my babies."

The men complied, holstering their sidearms.

"Folks, our work is nowhere near done. We've begun a campaign against the enablers, those commie libs who give aid and comfort to the coloreds, who somehow believe darkies are equal to us. They're providing sanctuary to the enemy."

Many people booed and hissed.

"There ain't no changing those traitors' minds. They're beyond redemption. So all we can do is put 'em out of their misery. One by one, until the job gets done. And may the good Lord have mercy on their lost souls. Know what, though, if our Savior gives these enablers a thumbs down, it's fine by me. How about you?"

Everyone screamed their approval.

"Let 'em burn in hell, Ms. Raven."

"Come on, let me strangle them real slow just like that Miles Davis fella said."

"Time for a hung Jewry!"

Raven laughed and clapped back at the crowd.

"We couldn't do any of this without your support—oh no, y'all, I sound like one of those PBS pansies, don't I. All of you paid ten thousand dollars each to attend tonight. We thank you from the very bottom of our rebel hearts. So, we have a silent auction going on right now. I want to see some cray, cray bids for genuine slave shackles, which were worn today by our guest of honor."

Perspiring heavily and hungry as an orphan, Doris' husband yelled, "Ms. Raven, I want to be the first to bid one-thousand dollars for those slave shackles."

Many guests laughed and huzzahed.

Raven leaned down to Chance.

"Who's that guy?"

"Doris' husband," Chance replied.

"Oh, yeah, right."

The dinner bell sounded.

"Let's eat, y'all," Raven said. "And don't forget we have a special presentation at ten p.m."

Holding two dinner plates, Doris' husband finally was turned loose on the buffet.

17

———————

Only fifteen minutes remained before the special event.

Megan, Jimmie, and Colt were busy stringing up Vlad to the wooden cross. Vlad was silent and offered no resistance. Megan brought seven three-foot lengths of braided polypropylene rope. As Colt and Jimmie held Vlad against the cross, Megan used three sections of rope to tie Vlad's right arm, then three sections for his left arm. She saved for last her tying Vlad's ankles to the vertical post of the cross.

"Okay, Riders of the Purple Sage, go get the spotlights and, for heaven's sake, make sure the extension cord is long enough," Megan said.

I got that from my Zane Gray Westerns, she reminded herself.

Colt nodded yes; Jimmie gave her a Nazi salute.

That idiot Jimmie doesn't want to live much longer, Megan thought.

"Meantime, I'll double check the knots, make sure our guest of horror is snug as a bed bug."

Zane Gray's cowpokes walked away.

"Did she say '*whore*', Colt?"

"'*Horror*', you moron."

Megan fussed with the knots.

Vlad whispered, "I know who you are, Megan. I met you at the Hangar last year. You seemed so wholesome and kind."

Megan didn't look at Vlad.

"Yeah, well, you didn't seem too impressed I was a lesbian."

"I am sorry, Megan. I am a recent convert to Islam, and there is no more zealous a follower than the converted. Please forgive me."

Megan paused with her knot adjustments.

"I think I actually believe you, Vlad."

He smiled warmly.

"Why are you participating in this evil spectacle? Has that woman got you under a Sapphic spell?"

Megan began retying the knots, starting with Vlad's left arm.

"I'm keeping busy here, don't want to call attention to my talking with you."

"Good idea, Megan. Please try to answer my question."

She exhaled.

"I admit I am very attracted to Raven. Never seen so much sexual energy wrapped up in one little package. Doesn't help, either, that I'm not that big of a fan of the coloreds."

Vlad gave her an understanding nod.

"A confession: I was introduced to Islam by a very attractive Black woman and her husband. Did her beauty sway me? Absolutely."

Megan smiled at Vlad.

"Thank you for your honesty. Makes me feel like less of an idiot."

She moved over to re-do the knots on Vlad's right arm.

"You are welcome, Megan."

"You know this isn't going to end well for you, right?"

"Oh, I am well aware of my chances of surviving this night."

Megan bent down and re-tied the knot at Vlad's ankle.

"I'm already regretting this, Vlad, but I think I can help you out."

"Barakallahu fik, may Allah bless you,"

"Thanks for the translation, pahdner," Megan said. "Here's the best I can do: disguised slip knots. Give 'em a good strong yank and you'll be free. You'll be on your own, Vlad. I can't risk doing any more."

"Will you be okay, after helping me like this?"

Megan smiled devilishly.

"That Maggie Thatcher was right about us—you can't trust the Oirish, we're all unrepentant liars. I can talk my way out of most any situation."

"Erin go Bragh."

"Till the end of time."

Megan stepped away from Vlad just as Jimmie and Colt returned with two spotlights, an outdoor power strip, and a hundred-foot extension cord.

"We have five minutes, no more, no less. Get a move on, boys."

"Yes, ma'am," Colt said.

Jimmie ignored Megan.

They busied themselves with setting up the spotlights.

Colt paused to ask, "He givin' ya any trouble, ma'am?"

"No trouble at all, and I'll neuter you if you call me ma'am again," Megan said.

"Yes, Miss Megan," Colt said, properly chastised.

While Colt and Jimmie were present, Vlad remained silent, kept his head lowered, and pretended to be disoriented.

"We're all done here, Miss Megan," Colt said. "All we gotta do is run the extension cord to an outlet by the veranda."

Megan nodded her approval.

"Excellent. Now, Colt, you stay by the power strip and wait for Chance's signal to light the cross, I mean, light *up* the cross."

"Humpf, don't you trust me to plug it in on time, *Miss Megan?*"

Megan put her hands on her hips.

"I wouldn't trust you to walk my dead cat, Jimmie boy."

"Go ahead, taco queen, call me 'boy' again. I double-dog dare you."

Jimmie had hit the ground twice today, and he didn't anticipate a third time. But the day wasn't over yet. Colt came up behind Jimmie and shoved his backside with a boot heel. Jimmie face-planted on the ground.

Colt unholstered his Browning semi-automatic pistol and aimed it at Jimmie, then said, "You ever disrespect Miss Megan again, and I'll blow your head off."

Still on his stomach, Jimmie reached behind his back to pull a Ruger LCR 9mm from his waistband.

Megan stomped her boot on Jimmie's hand and retrieved his pistol.

"No gun play, gentlemen. Get up off the ground, Jimmie."

He stood up and brushed himself off.

Megan handed him his Ruger.

"Put away that weapon. Same goes for you, Colt."

The young men complied.

Megan put her hand on Colt's shoulder.

"Thank you, darling, for sticking up for me. But you have to think out your impulses. Last thing our Raven wants is a shoot-out before the big show. Trust me, everything's gonna work out, sweet Colt."

Megan gave him a peck on his cheek.

Think I'm falling for a gay, Colt thought.

Colt and Megan sitting in a tree, K-I-S-S-I-N-G, Jimmie thought, as he smiled and raised his eyebrows.

Look at that, Jimmie had an unspoken wisecrack, Megan thought. Will wonders never cease.

"Let's huddle up, you two desperados," Megan said sternly.

Colt and Jimmie both said, "Yes, Miss Megan."

"Colt, you head to the veranda, locate Chance, wait for his signal—remember he'll take off his Stetson. Go on, vamoose!"

Colt took off running in the direction of the veranda.

"Jimmie, I'll race you to the stable. I'll even give you a head start. Beat me there, I'll give you a case of Natty."

Jimmie sprinted towards the stable.

"Eat my dust, ma'am."

Megan turned her head and gave Vlad a slight nod.

Vlad returned the nod.

18

———————

As Raven walked through the amped-up crowd, the band played "I Wish I Was in Dixie".

She stopped abruptly and turned to her guests.

Everything was in place. Though Raven could barely make out the wooden cross, she was confident Megan did her job. Chance stood off to the side, patiently waiting for her signal to illuminate the cross. Colt remained hidden behind azalea bushes; he maintained a clear sight line to Chance.

C'mon, Chance, let me light 'er up, Colt thought.

Let's get this thing going, Raven said to herself.

"Y'all, it's time for the big reveal," she announced.

A drunken woman yelled out, "Just like H Gay TV, Raven!"

Darn thief, I came up with that, Chance thought.

The crowd applauded loudly, though Doris' husband, juggling a glass of sweet tea and a dinner plate piled high with pie and cake, could only holler his approval. He wore a large white cloth napkin tucked into his open shirt collar.

"Doris, honey, would you wipe my mouth with the napkin? My face feels sticky."

Doris scoffed.

"Please stop eating off the plate with your mouth. So disgusting, you're embarrassing me."

She used his napkin to wipe peach filling and chocolate frosting off his mouth and chin.

Doris went over to the dessert table, grabbed a fork, then slid it into her husband's shirt pocket.

"They're called utensils, you tub of lard, give 'em a try sometimes."

Though his face reddened with anger, Doris' husband kept silent. He simply nodded yes.

Raven stood tall again on the black plywood box.

"Tonight's ceremony will be most exciting for y'all. I also hope and pray it will be real expensive for you. Just remember, this is all for a great and righteous cause."

Sensing they were getting lassoed to pony up more money, the guests' response was somewhat muted.

"Come on now, folks. Believe me, this will be money well spent. You can't see it right now, but there's a wooden cross over yonder. Tied up to that cross is a genuine Mandingo."

Doris yelled, "What cha got, Ken Norton over there?"

People laughed and cheered.

"No, not Ken Norton. Even better, y'all. We got ourselves a Black Muslim!"

The crowd returned to uproarious celebrating.

A few men wanted to fire their handguns but thought better of it.

Then someone asked, "Are we gonna barbecue the young buck?"

A hush came over the crowd.

"What? What'd I say?" the man asked.

Guests started talking quietly among themselves. Women could be heard saying "My word" and "Frightful" and "Looks like no dessert for me." Raven nodded to Chance, who then strode over to the loud-mouthed guest and put his arm around the man's shoulders.

"Merle here didn't mean to be such a stinky turd blossom. He's gotta learn to go easy on that Kentucky bourbon."

Most everyone turned their attention to Chance.

"Course we're not gonna barbecue that colored boy. We ain't

savages, y'all. No, we're the last of the white civilized world. Can I get an amen?"

People shouted "Amen" and raised their arms to heaven.

Chance gave the crowd his most alluring smile.

A woman yelled, "You're one lucky woman, Raven! Look at the smile on that man. I'm getting all hot and bothered."

"Preaching to the choir, Bernice," Raven said. "Now, here's the deal, y'all. For five thousand a lash, you get to use a bullwhip on our Mandingo. Look at it this way: you can check off another item on your bucket list."

Doris' husband threw his plate and glass into the azalea bushes, wiped his face with the cloth napkin, and stepped up.

"Miss Raven, I'll buy two lashes, one for me and one for Doris."

One of these days, I gotta get that man's name, Raven thought.

"As the coloreds say, don't go yanking my weave. You're sure, about you *and* Doris?"

Like a purple peacock with his tail fanned out, the man nodded his head yes in a regal manner.

"All righty then, do y'all want to warm up a little?" Raven asked.

"Don't think so. What kind of bullwhip?" Doris' husband inquired.

"Mustang Australian."

"One of our favorites. How long? Ten feet, I hope."

"Yes, sir. Ten feet it is."

"Can we borrow some gloves, Miss Raven?"

"Will Rough Rider Drivers work?"

"Perfect."

"Comfy using bullwhips?" Raven wondered.

He showed an evil grin, similar to that of Ted Bundy's.

"Oh we're expert floggers. You've see our home dungeon."

"TMI, my friend," Chance interjected.

The crowd laughed.

Doris' husband giggled.

"Anywho, what d'ya think of this: I'll give you fifty thousand dollars, five lashes for me, five for Doris."

"You have a deal," Raven exclaimed.

"As usual, make the check out to the Rebel Yell Historical Society?"

"Yes, sir."

He looked at his wife, who was standing unusually close to him—for once, she enjoyed the attention he brought to them.

"Doris, honey, make out a check for Miss Raven."

Doris smiled warmly at him, then said, "Yes, handsome."

She retrieved a checkbook from her Louis Vuitton purse and scribbled out a check while holding the checkbook against her husband's left shoulder.

Doris handed the check to Raven, who glanced at it quickly.

So that's his name, she thought.

"Hey, Miss Raven, is there room for anyone else with this whipping?" a young man asked.

Can't believe that boy owns a Ford dealership, Raven thought. So wealthy, so good looking ... oh, well, back to business.

"Sorry, Kenny, our Black Muslim Mandingo couldn't take much more than ten lashes from that Mustang Australian whip. We want to flog him, not filet him. Like Chance said, we ain't savages."

Besides, I get to finish off Vlad, Raven reminded herself.

"I can respect that, ma'am, maybe next time," Kenny said. "And besides, most of the folks are here for the spectacle."

"Agree on both counts. So what do you say we show you our guest of honor?" Raven said in an officious voice.

She nodded to Chance, who took off his Stetson.

Suddenly, the wooden cross lit up a good fifty yards away.

(Colt almost missed Chance's signal, as he was busy wiping off peach pie and sweet tea, compliments of Doris' husband.)

Raven turned and looked at the cross.

She raised her arms, then dropped them to her side.

Vlad was not on the cross.

The guest of honor somehow took an early leave of the festivities.

19

———————

Raven didn't say a word as she stood with her back to the crowd.

Almost everyone was as quiet as a pallbearer.

Except for one couple.

"Talk about disrupting my inner feng shui," Dead-Eye Dick opined.

(Dick's first cousin Sid poked out Dick's left eye with a sterling silver candelabra during a brawl at a family funeral.)

"To say nothing, love, of weakening our personal chi," Cutty said.

(Agatha's family and friends always called her "Cutty", though no one knew why.)

"True that, Cutty," Dead-Eye Dick replied. "More importantly, I feel really bad for Miss Raven."

"Don't you worry about Miss Raven," Cutty answered. "She's got Chance to console her."

Dead-Eye Dick lifted his eye patch and winked at Cutty with his milky left eye.

"Stop, Dick, you're getting me all humid like," Cutty chortled.

My followers—so understanding and so very weird, Raven thought.

"We've no need for a surprise pity party here," she said. "I'm just so dang sorry to let y'all down. Can't believe he scampered off like that."

Chance went into action, first putting his tree limb of an arm around his wife's shoulders and giving her a gentle hug.

He whispered to her, "Let me take care of this, okay?"

Struggling to hold back a cascade of tears, she nodded yes.

"Listen up, everybody," Chance said in a sonic booming voice. "This is how we make moonshine out of lunar rocks."

"Huh?" Merle said.

"It's a metaphor, you blockhead," Cutty said disdainfully.

"What'd y'all expect, a brave colored?" Chance asked. "Shoot, they's the most cowardly critters on the face of the earth—'cept maybe the Mexicans."

The crowd struck up a thunderstorm of laughter and cheers.

Getting them about where I want 'em, Chance thought.

"Don't worry, we're gonna find our Mandingo. Be real easy—go to the nearest briar patch, take a whiff, and he'll be right there."

Now everyone was clapping, even Doris and her husband, who remained deeply disappointed they weren't going to bullwhip a Black man.

"Whatcha got in mind, you hunk of a cowboy?" seventy-four-year-old Ifla asked.

"You're thinking with your Georgia O'Keefe again, young lady," eighty-year-old Rosie said with a soupçon of playfulness.

"Whatever, dear, she's never let me down before," Ifla answered.

"All right, you two, remember you're both Ladies of the *Invisible Empire*," Chance interjected.

Ifla scoffed.

"What's that supposed to mean, me and Rosie are not to be seen or heard from?"

Ifla's flushed face was framed by short hair as white as a New England snow drift.

Clearly, she meant business.

Chance immediately walked back his sexist remark.

"Ifla, Rosie, sorry about that. Sometimes, I'm one full bubble off plumb."

He smiled at the two elderly women.

"Chance Doyle, I do believe you could get Mother Teresa all hot and bothered," Ifla said. "Just don't be so dismissive of women. We can be every bit as smart and clever as you men. If you don't believe me, take a gander at your wife."

Raven looked at Chance.

"Ifla's right, you know, dear husband."

Chance tipped his black Stetson to his wife.

"Guilty as charged, y'all. And I want to assure everyone of one thing: if we find him before the party's over, the show will go on as planned.

"I would think so, Chance," Doris said frostily.

Her husband nodded in agreement.

"Yes, ma'am, for sure. We have our ranch hands out looking for him right now."

"If'n you don't find him, what do we get as compensation?" Rosie asked warily.

Things are going due south right fast, Chance thought. Sweet Jesus, why'd I make that crack about Ifla and Rosie keeping quiet?

"We have an American flag with a target painted on it. We'll nail the flag upside down on the cross, and y'all can use it for target practice. Doris, you and your husband can then bullwhip it to shreds. In fact, Colt, get on over to the ranch house shed and retrieve the flag. Do it right now, boy."

"Yes, sir," Colt answered hesitantly. He scampered off in the direction of the shed.

Earle, Chief Deputy Sheriff for Hillsborough County, chuckled as he checked the ammo magazine to his Sig Sauer 9mm.

"Chance, won't the horses get all riled up?" he asked.

Raven answered Earle's question.

"Don't worry about it, not like they haven't heard gunshots before. And really, this is the least I can do for y'all."

"I'll say," Rosie said sarcastically.

Raven and Chance felt it slipping away.

Luckily, Colt showed up with the American flag.

"Good job, boy," Chance said. "Now go nail the flag upside down on the cross and be quick about it."

Colt didn't move.

"Sorry, sir, I won't further desecrate the U.S. flag by nailing it to a cross upside down. That's for signaling emergencies only. 'Sides, my sis is in the Navy and my big brother is a Marine. My father did two tours in Vietnam. No, sir. I will not do what you ask. Find someone else, please."

Chance slapped Colt to the ground.

"You ever disobey me again, I'll make you disappear right quick, *boy*."

Chief Deputy Sheriff Earle holstered his Sig Sauer pistol and moved between Chance and Colt.

"That's enough of that, Chance. You should know better than to beat on a youngin' half your size."

Chance glared at the chief deputy.

"I'll handle Colt any way I've a mind to, Earle."

"I respect that, but keep in mind as well that this ain't Jonestown. We all support the Cause. We all see you and Raven as our leaders. But we aren't about to drink the Kool-Aid, my friend."

Chance didn't respond. Seems like Earle's running a power play, now don't it, he thought.

Earle helped up Colt and patted dust off of him.

"If I were you, Colt, I'd apologize to Chance, then make myself scarce."

With tears falling down his cheeks, Colt said, "Mr. Doyle, I am sorry for disobeying you. I hope you can understand why I did it."

Unlike Raven, Chance never let his temper get the best of him, at least not for too long.

He spit on the ground, then smiled.

"Don't worry about it, son, I accept your apology. Now scram."

Colt moved as fast as a hermit crab scuttling away from a hungry blue heron.

20

———————

"Shootin' up the American flag is all well and good, but why can't we whip on that grouchy butler of yours? He's old as dirt, let's send 'em on his way," Brownie asked.

She stood rigid and upright in an attempt to make her five-foot frame stand tall in the hearts of people around her.

(Brownie was born into a Klan family, suggesting even racists are capable of an inside joke.)

Raven stomped her cowboy boot on the ground.

"Ventley has been the family house-colored for nigh on fifty years. He's no field-colored. He's too important in our home. I value him almost as much as my dogs. Do you feel me, Brownie? You better, if you know what's good for you."

The silence was as smothering as Florida's summertime humidity.

Eventually, Brownie responded.

"Yes, Raven. I feel you. Sorry, it was just an idea."

Raven stomped her boot again.

"And it was a stupid ...."

The sound of a hammer banging interrupted her.

While Chance supervised, Megan nailed the upside-down American flag to the wooden cross.

Chance had whispered to her, "You're already in real deep with Raven, so do a better job this time."

Megan simply nodded yes.

Chance turned toward the crowd.

"Let's get the lead out, you sharp shooters. And Doris, I'll have Jimmie go get your bullwhip and gloves from the stable."

Chance nodded to Jimmie, who took off for the stable as fast as an Arizona roadrunner.

"Come on now, folks, who's going first?" Chance asked.

No one moved. No one spoke—not even chatty Dead-Eye Dick or Cutty. Just crickets, real and metaphorical.

"Is there some kind of problem, y'all?" Raven asked.

Crickets once more.

Then Earle spoke.

"Yes, Raven, we have a problem."

"Go ahead, Earle, let's hear it," Raven said with a sigh.

The chief deputy was fifty, tall, and built like an NFL middle linebacker on steroids. He earned a reputation for being fair and decent, though people knew he could be extremely dangerous if bump came to bulldoze.

"Raven and Chance, we think we should get our money back," Earle said with confidence behind his words. "Shooting up Old Glory and whipping it into shreds just don't twang our buds, if y'all catch our drift."

Chance stepped forward and stood about three feet from Earle.

"Tell me if you heard this one, good buddy. The Lone Ranger and Tonto got set upon by a passel of Apaches. Lone Ranger, he decides to take off toward a canyon. Tonto follows after him. Bad decision on Lone Ranger's part, turns out it's a box canyon. They're trapped, and the Apaches are fast approaching. Lone Ranger says, 'Well, Tonto, what're we gonna do?' Tonto says, 'What you mean 'we', white man?'"

Both Earle and Chance laughed, but the tension remained.

"That's a good'n Chance, really is. And I get the point of your little joke. However, I assure you, we're unified in wanting our money back. Tell you what, though, just give us back eight thousand each, I mean, we ate a fine meal, enjoyed the open bar, and the bluegrass band was tall cotton, indeed. Oh, one other little thing: tear up right quick Doris and her husband's check. We don't rightly see how you can keep their fifty thousand dollars."

This time, Raven stepped forward and stood next to her husband.

"Pfft. Is that what you want, Doris? If it is, fine by me. But don't think I'm gonna go with you anymore to Ybor City and help you find subs. And you can forget Sunday brunch here for a whole month of Sundays."

Doris held back tears then said, "The brunch ban stings the worst, Raven. You know how I love your biscuits and red-eye gravy. And thank you very much for letting everyone know about my little pastime. Real nice of you, just real nice. But yes, you need to tear up that check or I'll stop payment on it."

Raven gave Doris a predatory smile. "No problem, Doris."

Raven pulled the check from her back pocket and tore it into tiny pieces, then threw the pieces in the air as if they were confetti. A few pieces landed in Doris' blonde hair.

"That's done and duster, y'all," Raven said. "Now let's see with a show of hands who wants their money back."

Almost everyone raised their hands, including Merle, who owned a large strawberry farm near Riverview and was very much in love with Raven.

"Sorry, Raven," he said with sadness in his voice.

Raven crossed her arms.

"Don't worry about it, Merle. You're just being led around by Deputy Barney Fife there."

Chief Deputy Earle smiled broadly.

"Well, Raven, you know what me and Barney Fife say, 'You gotta nip it ... in the bud.'"

If Raven had a gasket, she was about to blow it. And Chance knew it. He leaned down and whispered something to Raven, who turned and stared at the cross with the upside-down American flag attached. After an awkward minute or two of silence passed, Raven then faced the crowd.

"Fine and dandy, y'all, everyone gets *ten thousand* back. Each. And not eight thousand, *ten thousand*. Chance and I are happy to have hosted y'all for a nice buffet dinner outside on a beautiful night—look at all those stars, makes me feel as if heaven's looking over us, taking names, willing to sort it out later."

"Thank you, Raven," Doris said.

Raven gave her a squinty smile.

"No worries, girl. And that goes for you, too, Barney."

Chief Deputy Earle tipped his white cowboy hat to her, turned around, and left the festivities.

Soon enough, that man's gonna get his, right proper, Raven thought.

"We'll send out your checks tomorrow, folks, or my name isn't Raven Lisibet Doyle. Okay now, time to call it a night. Drive safe."

Raven and Chance remained on the veranda. Caterers busied themselves with packing up the food and bagging the trash. Bartenders were just as busy breaking down the bar. Dixie Daze was almost done with stacking instruments and equipment onto loading dollies.

Chance held Raven's hand.

"So there's that, I suppose." she said wistfully.

21

———————

Chance and Raven sat in the grand room of the mansion. The dogs stretched out near Raven.

"When do you want me to take care of Earle?"

Raven smiled at Chance in a most evil manner.

"Not for a couple months, I want him to let his guard down."

Chance chuckled.

"Yes, ma'am. Execution style? Set up the BarraCubas or the Bavarians for the hit?"

She reached up and gently pinched his left ear lobe.

"Yes, execute him. Biker gang's a good idea. Go with the BarraCubas. They won't mind, it'll elevate their status in Tampa, what with their being an all-chick biker gang and all."

"Yes, ma'am. What should we do about Colt and Megan? Can't let Colt get away with that insolence, and Megan either did a lousy job tying up Vlad or she did it on purpose."

Raven seemed lost in thought.

"Hello?" Chance asked.

"Sorry, just thinking. I'm on the same page with you about Colt and Megan. Take 'em with you tonight when you get rid of Jimmie. That'll shake them up. When you get back, have fun with Megan. It'll be your one and only time with her."

Chance raised his carefully trimmed black eyebrows.

"Care to explain?"

Raven undid the top button of Chance's black Columbia sports shirt, slipped in her hand, and massaged his well-defined chest.

"What's up, hon, is that I promise not to get jealous when you're with that Irish cutie. All I ask is when you wake up in the morning, love me harder."

Chance gathered her in his arms and kissed her passionately.

"Oh, I'll love you harder—only way I'm gonna keep you. But what else is on your mind?"

"You really understand me, Chance Doyle. We don't need Colt and Megan once we're through with Reed and Jake. Get rid of them next week."

"Aye, aye, Gunny. Dump 'em in the usual place?"

"Hmm, I think so. Are you keeping your map up to date? We need to be ready in a flash in case some Nosy Nellie comes snooping around those woods."

"All up to date and in our safe."

Raven stood on her toes to bite playfully on Chance's lower lip.

"My man, you truly are the bestest. Now don't you worry about what happened tonight. Yeah, we'll take a financial hit, but we have more money than the Jews. Our buddy Earle made his move, and he almost pulled it off. He didn't, did he. No room to feel sorry for ourselves. Time to focus on Friday night. Agree?"

Chance gave her his Olympic gold-medal smile, reserved only for Raven.

"I want you right now, dear husband. Let's go upstairs and put this night to bed, so to speak."

Before the couple walked upstairs, Raven stepped out on the veranda and spotted Megan and Colt standing together in the shadows.

Raven waved at them, then blew a kiss to Megan.

"No need to hide, you two. You ain't in any trouble. Goodnight, sweethearts."

Ventley the butler held open the French doors for Raven. The black labs greeted her with howls and happy prancing.

Outside, Colt turned to Megan and asked, "Believe her, Megan?"

"Nope, not one word."

"Me neither. Listen, I gotta talk with you, okay?

"Of course, Colt."

"Thanks, I've grown partial to you. Sissy ain't gonna be happy if she finds out. Don't much care, I think you're beautiful and real sweet. Doesn't matter if you like women. I think I'm falling for you."

Megan put her hand on his right cheek.

"If I ever could be persuaded to take up with a man, it would be with you, Colt. You're in a relationship, though. You aren't going to betray your lady."

She kissed him lightly on the lips.

Colt gave her a gentlemanly hug.

"Megan, if Sissy and I don't work out, I'll come a calling."

"Fair enough, darling."

"I have something else to talk with you about."

"What would that be?"

Colt paused to look around, making sure no one was listening.

"I know where Vlad is hiding."

22

———————

Reed climbed out of her king bed. She was barely awake. It was seven a.m. on Tuesday. Jake was still asleep—he didn't get home until four a.m. Fortunately, no problems arose at Namaste the previous night. Reed looked at her slumbering husband. He was halfway under the white down duvet, with his left leg sticking out. Reed loved his broad shoulders, bare chest, muscular arms and legs, and egg carton abdominals. Since he was asleep, she was denied gazing at his deep blue eyes, which always reminded her of the Caribbean Sea at high noon.

Gonna let my man sleep longer, but time for me to face the new day, Reed thought.

Wearing only lime green footies adorned with white swans, she padded into her walk-in closet and slipped into a rose and tan flounce kimono robe.

Must ... have ... coffee, she chanted to herself.

Reed walked into the island kitchen and started the electric tea kettle.

She carefully measured out seven flat scoops of Lavazza coffee. She had ground the whole beans before going to bed, knowing Jake would be sleeping in this morning.

The tea kettle whistled.

Reed promptly poured the boiling water over the aromatic coffee grounds in the French press. She placed the plunger atop the glass cylindrical cantor. She waited four minutes, then slowly plunged down, trapping the spent grounds at the bottom, and leaving rich Arabica coffee ready to pour.

"Spare a cup of joe?"

Reed turned and saw Ravel standing in the living room.

Except for wearing a pair of Ray-Ban Wayfarer sunglasses, she was completely naked.

Ravel kept her petite figure in great shape, though she still had scars on her chest from Russian mobster Victor Petrov caning her while he held her prisoner.

Her unbrushed short black hair resembled an out-of-control prison riot.

"Ravel, can I offer you a robe?"

Reed tried to deal positively with Ravel's occasional outlandish behavior.

"Only if it's the robe you're wearing," Ravel snapped back.

Reed smiled benevolently.

"Young lady, I will not allow you to gallivant around our home wearing nothing but sunglasses and a smile."

Ravel pretended to pout.

"What's the big deal? I'm Swiss, we are very open minded about nudity. I hardly think Jake would care; besides it might put some ideas in your pretty little head."

She slid her sunglasses down her ski-slope nose so Reed could admire her deep purple eyes.

Reed shook her head, but she was only slightly annoyed.

"There's no smoke on the water or fire in the sky over here, sweetie. Jake is more than enough for me. Now, march into your bedroom and put on the bathrobe we gave you for Christmas. Only then will you get your cup of joe."

"Fine, but just try not to stare at my magnificent bottom."

With that, Ravel turned and slowly retreated to her bedroom.

Such an imp, and no, I will not look at her bum, Reed thought.

Ravel returned modeling a fluffy white bathrobe and still wearing her shades.

"Better?"

"Much," Reed said. "You look ready for a day at the Hard Rock Spa."

Ravel took off her sunglasses and slid them into a robe pocket.

"I wish, but we do need to go back to the Hard Rock—get a deep tissue massage, a facial, mani-pedi, soak in the whirlpool, sip on green tea, you know, the whole shebang."

Reed smiled warmly at Ravel, then poured her a cup of coffee.

"Sounds wonderful, but next time we bring Jake, deal?

"Long as you're paying, I've no problem with taking the big lug with us. Speaking of said lug, I see you made your own coffee again— and by the way, it's delicious—does that mean he has the day off?"

Ravel was aware of Reed and Jake's arrangement: Reed wasn't raised to cook and clean and launder; since Jake was, he gladly took on the chores.

"No, it does not mean that at all. He didn't get in until very late, and he needs his sleep. I'm not going to wake up my man to make coffee for me. I know how to use a French press, thank you very much. However, if he wants to fix me supper before he goes to Namaste—I'm thinking grilled salmon, no more than six ounces, a loaded baked potato, and sautéed asparagus spears with asiago cheese crumbles— then who I am to thwart his culinary magic."

"Haven't had breakfast, have you?" Ravel asked.

"No, I haven't. I guess I was waiting for Jake to ...."

"Um, huh?"

Both women laughed.

"You busted me, all right. It's difficult to admit I'm dependent on Jake. So what do you say we cut up some cantaloupe and strawberries? We're independent women, right?"

"Absolutely, love."

As she often did, Ravel had let herself in the penthouse late last night. Since Reed was quite protective of the nomadic Ravel, she gave the Swiss genius her own bedroom and en suite. Ravel spent most of her nights at her lover Sierra's condominium on Harbour Island. But the couple had argued, centering on Ravel's low level of commitment to the relationship, so Ravel retreated to Reed and Jake's apartment.

In many respects, the penthouse was Ravel's primary domicile. What few clothes she had, she kept at the penthouse. When she washed her laundry there, she included Reed and Jake's as well. Occasionally, she stopped at the immense farmer's market on Hillsborough Avenue at dawn, gathering a cornucopia of fresh mangos, avocados, watermelon, cantaloupes, strawberries, cukes, tomatoes, and peppers of various colors and heat intensity. Since she drove a red Porsche Boxster, she limited her purchases to those which could be accommodated in the Boxster's small rear trunk and slightly larger front trunk, or what Boxster enthusiasts call a "frunk." She adhered to the lone household rule: no overnight guests, not even Swedish Sierra.

The only rub was Ravel competing with Jake over who was first to swim in the terrace lap pool.

(Ravel often bested Jake by doing laps at five or six a.m., which is when she normally arrived at the penthouse.)

When it came to the kitchen, Ravel knew her way around far better than Reed.

"Looking for this, darling?"

Ravel held up a five-inch Santoku knife.

Reed chuckled, "Yeah, actually I was. Thanks."

She sliced open a cantaloupe, scooped out the innards, separated the fruit from the rind, and cut the sweet musky melon into bite-size chunks.

Ravel occupied herself with lopping off the tops of the strawberries, then slicing them in precisely the same width.

"Off with their heads!" she exclaimed.

"Lewis Carroll's Queen of Hearts?" Reed asked.

"Ha! You bet. My life parallels *Alice's Adventures in Wonderland.*"

She stole a glance at Reed, whose robe opened enough to show cleavage.

"Keep staring, Ravel, and you might cut off a finger."

Incredible peripheral vision on that woman, Ravel said to herself.

"Guess it's my turn to get busted," Ravel said, as she returned to guillotining the innocent, though tasty, strawberries.

The women filled three blue and white ceramic bowls. The third bowl would be for Jake, once he awakened. Ravel grabbed royal blue cloth napkins and salad forks, then set them on hemp place mats at the dining room table. Reed took two skinny cans of San Pellegrino sparkling water from the refrigerator. She also got whipped cream from the fridge and put a healthy dollop on top of each bowl of fruit.

Reed joined Ravel at the Petra dining room table, whose polished brown and black stone slices, cut from fossilized trees in the Philippines, formed a tessellation resembling a Rauschenberg abstract.

Instead of a buffet next to the table, Reed placed a five-foot high bookshelf containing her fifty-volume set of Harvard Classics.

Uncharacteristic of Reed, she brought her phone to the table.

"So," she said.

"So," Ravel answered.

"Have a favor to ask you."

"Name it and it shall be done, oh Great Queen of My Heart."

Reed set down her salad fork and wiped her mouth with the cloth napkin.

"You're just so funny, Ravel...funny in the head. Seriously, I want to arrange a lunch today with Raven Doyle."

While chewing a mouthful of cantaloupe and strawberries, Ravel said, "What am I now, your factotum? Why can't you call the witch yourself?"

Reed smiled kindly at her.

"No, you little macaron, I don't want you to call her. It's just that the only phone number I have is to her dominatrix business ...."

"Wait, what?"

"Cool your jets, woman. Yes, she's a dominatrix. She claims it's only a hobby."

"Very interesting. What's her dom name?"

"Miss Ravenous."

"Works for me."

"Cut it out. Please. I'd like you to find her personal phone number, the one reserved for only select callers. It's real important Raven sees I can break through her firefall."

"Firewall."

"What?"

"Firefall is an old country rock band from Colorado. You meant 'firewall', which is a computer security device, essentially a barrier between a private internal network and the public internet."

"Oh, well. Thank you for that clarification. I really don't mind being corrected by you."

"Double ha! You most certainly *hate* being corrected by anyone! Anyhoo, how about I grab my laptop and see if I can locate Little Miss Bondage."

Reed patted Ravel's hand.

"You're a peach. Thank you."

Ravel hopped out of the buffalo leather chair and practically ran to her bedroom to retrieve her prized laptop. She relished every chance to impress Reed with her computer wizardry. Ravel took less than three minutes to find Raven's private phone number. She danced across the keyboard, generating the clickety clackety sound of a Geiger counter gone Godzilla.

"There you go, sweetums."

Ravel showed Raven's private number to Reed.

"You're the best, Ravel."

"Hey, if it's on the Net, I'll find it. Have I earned a kiss?"

"Yes, of course."

Reed gave Ravel a dainty peck on the cheek.

She picked up her phone.

"Time to make a call to my current fav arch nemesis."

Ravel giggled then clapped gleefully.

23

"Raven, I'm so happy we could get together on such short notice," Reed said chirpily.

"Overjoyed you called me, but, you know, you *did* promise we'd lunch," Raven said. "Have to admit, I was kinda surprised you called me on my super-secret Batphone—only Commissioner Gordon uses that line."

Reed laughed softly, then spoke just as softly.

"I wasn't comfortable calling your dominatrix line, which was the only number you gave me on New Year's Eve."

Raven raised her micro-bladed black eyebrows.

"So how'd you find my private line?"

"Sorry, if I told you ...."

"Good luck killing me. Anyway, no big dealio. Let's not turn this into an MMA cage match—not yet, at least."

"It is a bit early, isn't it? I like to think patience is always rewarded, eventually."

She and Raven sat in the Fountain Grille, inside the Safety Harbor Resort and Spa. It was noon on Tuesday.

The spa was on the far northwestern shore of Tampa Bay in Pinellas County.

For better than sixty years, the Safety Harbor Spa provided five-star services: diet and exercise programs, massages, facials, herbal wraps, and all levels of yoga. There were swimming pools, whirlpools, saunas, steam rooms, a polar plunge, and a top-notch tennis facility.

However, the spa stood out because it sat above natural mineral springs that Spanish conquistador Hernando de Soto discovered in 1539 and named Manantial de Espírítu Santo, or Spring of the Holy Spirit. Believing the mineral springs held healing powers, people from all over the world, including European and Middle Eastern royalty, star athletes, and pop celebrities, arrived for week-long stays at the spa.

Today, in great contrast to the vampy outfit she wore on New Year's Eve, Raven paired a white Ralph Lauren Polo dress shirt with tan slacks and dark brown ankle boots.

All bidness I am, she vowed to herself.

Reed put thought into her outfit as well. She chose a blue and white tie-dye sarong dress that showed off her bare shoulders and shapely figure. Naturally, with a sarong she didn't wear a bra.

Time to give this shady lady a taste of her own mad medicine, Reed told herself.

Woman has a great body, Raven thought.

"Wasn't that so much fun on New Year's Eve!" she exclaimed.

"It really was a grand time," Reed replied. "I'm not sure I've met someone as fascinating as you: so bright and confident and, don't take this the wrong way, beautiful."

Raven paused for a few seconds, as if she were gauging Reed's sincerity.

"Gosh, I don't think I've had another woman, on my level anyway, tell me that. Women, we are *sooo* competitive with each other. I guess all I can say is we're sorta like twins."

In your dreams and my nightmares, Reed thought.

A server approached their table.

She was in her mid-fifties and of Eastern European descent.

"Good afternoon, ladies, can we start you off with something to drink?"

"Yes, Katarzyna, but you first, Raven. Remember, my treat."

"Katarzyna, what a lovely name," Raven said. "Where are you from?"

"Poland, ma'am. Miss Reed is one of only a few who addresses me as 'Katarzyna'. Most everyone else just calls me 'Katherine'."

Poland, wouldn't you know it, Raven thought disdainfully.

"Well, Katherine, I'd like a gin and tonic. Sorry, but I'm very fussy about my cocktails. Please use three ounces of London dry gin, Beefeaters will do, but I prefer Bombay Sapphire. Then add four ounces of Schweppes tonic water, and a splash of lime juice, ice, and a lime *wedge*. Hot to trot, Miss Polka Dot?"

Katarzyna wrote down all of Raven's instructions.

"Very good, ma'am. And Miss Reed, your usual, Saratoga sparkling spring water, no ice?"

"Yes, please."

Katarzyna quickly stepped away.

"Looks as if you've been here before."

"Yes, Jake and I have been members for years."

Raven leaned forward.

"Oooh, members, no less. Very impressive."

Reed smiled.

"We come here every chance we get, though our obligations tend to keep us away from this oasis."

"Hmm, your obligations. Do they include enabling the poor, the downtrodden, the societal detritus of all colors of the rainbow?"

Reed smiled again.

"My, such big words for such a tiny woman."

"Ain't the size of the bitch in a fight, it's all about the size of the fight in the bitch. Tell me, love, do you suspect we're gonna end up pulling out each other's hair?"

"That why you keep your hair in a pixie cut? It's darling, by the way, and makes it tricky to grab a handful, *love*."

"Ha!" Raven said much too loudly.

Katarzyna returned with the drink order, just in time to calm the gathering squall.

She walked with a slight limp.

"Knee still hurts, doesn't it?" Reed asked.

"Only when I put weight on it," Katarzyna replied stoically.

She looks a solid two-sixty, those pierogis will do it to ya, Raven thought as she sipped her gin and tonic.

"Exactly as ordered. Compliments to the bartender."

"Actually, I prepared your cocktail because I wanted it to be perfect."

Raven took a second, larger sip.

"Then compliments to you, sugar."

"Thank you, ma'am. And are you ladies ready to order your food?"

"Yes, we are ready," Reed said. "Raven, what will you have?"

"Oh, I'm game for anything."

Bet you are, Reed thought.

"Then let's both have Salmon Athena."

"What does Salmon Athena entrail?"

Nope, not gonna bite, Reed thought.

"It's so yummy. It's poached Alaskan salmon. Caught, not farmed, on a bed of Greek orzo mixed with tomatoes, spinach, feta, and red onion, then sprinkled with lemon juice."

"Sounds wonderful, but what's Greek orzo?" Raven asked.

"I only recently discovered orzo. It's a short-cut pasta made with durum wheat semolina, which is higher in protein than your regular old wheat flour."

Geesh, I almost wish I hadn't asked Julia Child, Raven thought.

Raven finished her gin and tonic.

Drinks like a thirsty barracuda, Reed noted to herself.

Raven held up her empty glass and waved it at Katarzyna, who nodded yes to her.

"I say Salmon Athena for everyone!" Raven exclaimed.

"Yes, ma'am, and I'll bring you another gin and tonic."

"Thank you, Kat."

"And bring some bread with that gin and tonic, right pronto," Raven said loudly.

A portly Hispanic man, wearing a white spa robe and blue rubber slides, sat next to Reed and Raven's table. He looked disapprovingly at Raven, who stared right back at him.

"Look, El Porko, before you get all high and mighty on me, try closing your bathrobe—your junk's showing," Raven said angrily.

"Que?" the man asked.

"Su bata de baño," Raven answered. "Cierra su bata de baño, ahora!"

The man glanced down, then immediately closed his robe.

"Pendejo," Raven said in total disgust. "Guy doesn't like me talking loud, but he has no problem flashing us with his tiny pee-pee. Ay, caramba! Why can't these brownies just go back to Mexico or wherever?"

Temper, temper, Raven Doyle, Reed thought.

She didn't respond to Raven's diatribe. Instead, Reed took sips of her water, quietly appalled that some people have become so open about their bigotry. Katarzyna returned with the second gin and tonic and the requested basket of bread.

"Now that's what I'm talking about," Raven almost shouted. "Remember, sweetie, bring me another in five minutes."

Katarzyna smiled.

"The bread or the cocktail, ma'am?"

Raven squinted at her.

"Well, if you're gonna be a smarty pants, bring both."

"Yes, ma'am."

Katarzyna walked away.

Raven leaned forward with both elbows on the table. She took a hearty pull from her cocktail, paused, then took another drink.

"So, what's on your mind today? I mean, you're cute as a button, and I dig hanging with you, but this doesn't seem much like two gals having lunch together and talking fashion, sports, and animal husbandry."

Reed leaned forward, putting both elbows on the table as well.

"I wanted to mention two people I'm looking for, maybe get your help. Interested?"

Raven clawed a slice of the bread and viciously pecked at it.

"Mmm ... still warm. Yeah, sure, I'm interested. Talk to me."

Reed sipped more of her water.

"Remember Megan, the Irish bartender at the Hangar? You gave her a pretty impressive kiss on New Year's Eve."

Raven smiled lasciviously.

"Aw, Reed O'Hara is jealous I didn't kiss *her* like that."

Then Raven frowned.

"Of course, I remember sweetie pie Megan. I mean really, Reed, I was buzzed last Saturday night, not stoned drunk."

She quaffed the rest of her gin and tonic, put her small fingers inside the highball glass, clawed out the lime wedge, then bit into it.

"Megan's missing, Raven. Haven't heard from her in two days. I've been asked to find her."

"Passive voice."

"Excuse me?"

"You used passive voice. Who asked you to find Megan? Know for certain it isn't a boyfriend. Probably that eurotrash restaurant manager, right?"

"Can't say, but I'm bothered you seem interested only in who employed me to locate her. Don't you care that she's missing? Do you know where she is?"

Katarzyna approached the table with Raven's gin and tonic.

"Right on time," Raven said gleefully.

She took a thirsty drink of her cocktail.

"Relax, Reed. Of course, I care about Megan. And I know exactly where she is: at my home, on the ranch, you know, where the gators and opossum roam."

Ravel has got it right: we *are* lost in a Deep South wacky wonderland, Reed thought.

"Is Megan there of her own accord? Can she leave whenever she wants?"

Raven drank the rest of her gin and tonic.

She then smiled like Cardinal Richelieu, or at least like Charlton Heston's take on Richelieu's diabolical smile.

"What, afraid I put some kind of a spell on our girl? Well, I haven't. There's no need to go all voodoo hoodoo on her. She's free to go anytime she wants. But—and this is *sooo* important—she doesn't want to leave, okay? She has seen the light, and she is totally invested in what I stand for."

She's nuttier than a can of cashews, Reed thought.

"And what exactly do you stand for, Raven?"

"Simple, love. Superiority in all things. Complete blood harmony. Re-uniting the good people in Florida first, then the rest of the country, state by state. Our goal is to make the stars and bars shine again."

"Stars and bars, huh? Are we talking about Old Glory or the Dixie flag?"

Raven gave Reed her version of Katy Perry's protuberant blue eyes.

"You cut me to the quick, Reed O'Hara, I'm a patriot, not a seditionist. We intend to make Old Glory worthy again of our Christian patriotism."

Darn it, I let her off the hook about Megan, Reed thought.

"What do you get, Reed, when you join politics with religion?"

"I shudder to think of the possibilities."

"Don't be a wimp. What you get is a new crusade to take back Jerusalem, D.C."

"And how did those last crusades work out?"

"Oh, we're gonna learn from the past. Guarantee it."

Katarzyna returned with dinner bowls of Salmon Athena, along with more fresh bread and butter.

"Looks and smells yummy for the tummy, I must say," Raven said.

Katarzyna smiled proudly.

"Another gin and tonic, ma'am?"

"You bet," Raven said, as she used a soup spoon to scoop together chunks of salmon and orzo.

"Right away, Miss Raven, I'll be back in a jiffy with your cocktail."

"Say, Katherine, check this out," Raven said gleefully.

"I bet złoty to pączki that you don't know 'jiffy' is an astrophysical measurement of how long light takes to travel a distance of one femtometer, which is a millionth of a millionth of a millimeter. Just to put it in perspective, my Polish friend, there are about three hundred thousand billion jiffies in a second."

"Fascinating, ma'am," Katarzyna said unconvincingly.

"Thought you'd find that illuminating. So, I think you best recalibrate how quickly you'll return with my drink."

Katarzyna's thin smile was more Vermeer than Da Vinci.

"Would five minutes be acceptable?"

"You betcha!"

The robed Hispanic gentleman again looked disapprovingly at Raven.

She simply extended a middle finger salute to him.

"'Złoty to pączki'? Reed said. "Polish version of dollars to donuts?"

"Yup," Raven uttered in mid-chew.

"At least Katarzyna didn't use zeptosecond."

"Ha! Shortest unit of time ever measured. Did you just Google that, O'Hara?"

Reed gave her a smile that would have made Leonardo da Vinci or DiCaprio proud.

"Let's simply agree Victoria isn't the only woman with secrets," she said.

The two women were almost done with their entrees when Katarzyna returned with Raven's gin and tonic.

"Thanks, Kat, but you're one minute tardy."

"My apologies, ma'am."

"No worries."

Raven drank twice from her cocktail.

"Now *that's* how you clear the palette, yes indeedy."

"Looks as if you enjoyed the Salmon Athena, so would you like to try the chocolate tuxedo bomb for dessert," Reed asked.

Raven almost did a spit take with her gin and tonic.

"A tuxedo *bomb*, huh? Sounds fancy. But no, I'll pass. Gotta head out shortly."

"In that case, I want to mention another person I'm looking for, all right?"

"Aren't you the busy private investigator? How do you find time to practice the law and run your nightclub?"

"It's pretty much like juggling lit sticks of dynamite, but I find a way to make it work."

"Well then, ask away about this other person."

"His name is Vlad. He is the younger brother to Andre, who heads up security at Namaste."

"Um huh, go on."

"Vlad is also missing. In fact, he was kidnapped in the early hours of New Year's Day in the parking lot of La Mesa coffee shop over on Columbus in Tampa. We fully intend to find him. Alive. And well. Do you have any idea where Vlad might be?"

Raven finished her gin and tonic.

She blinked just for a moment.

"Now why on earth would you think I have any friggin' idea where this Vlad person might be? Colored boy probably couldn't make his vig. Who knows?"

Reed poured the rest of the Saratoga water into her goblet.

"Now, Raven, how did you know Vlad is Black?"

Raven blinked again.

"Because Andre is colored."

The two women stared at each other.

She who speaks first, loses, Reed thought.

"I don't want to play this game anymore," Raven said with a surly tone.

Score one for the good guys, Reed thought.

"No worries, Raven. But this hardly is a game we're playing. There is a life at stake. We simply must find Vlad, yet you don't seem to want to help."

Raven scoffed.

"You know a lot of people around here," Reed said. "I suspect our networks do not overlap very much. Should you hear anything, please call me, all right?"

Oh, our networks overlap far more than you realize, Raven chortled to herself.

"Sure, no problem, Reed. If I hear anything, I'll call you first thing. Hey, we're still on for Friday night, aren't we?"

"Yes, we are, Raven. And if you don't mind, please have Megan contact me. I want to reassure my client that she's safe and sound."

"Yeah, sure, whatever."

Katarzyna approached their table.

"I assumed you didn't want dessert, you rarely do. Here's the check,

Miss Reed."

Reed quickly scanned the check, then handed the server two hundred-dollar bills.

"No change, my friend, and please, call me Reed'"

Katarzyna positively beamed.

"Thank you, Reed, that really helps."

"You're welcome, but get that knee looked at."

"I will. Promise."

Katarzyna happily swanned away.

"So," Reed said.

"*Sooo* what," Raven answered.

"Our lunch has been fun and enlightening."

"Gonna write this lunch off, hmm?"

"Goodness, Raven, this was strictly social. I feel we've gotten to know each other better."

"Maybe a little bit, yes."

Raven stared at Reed's breasts.

"You okay to drive, Raven?"

"Hmm, what? Oh, no, I certainly am not okay to drive. I got Chance waiting outside in his truck that's 'bout the size of the USS *Alabama*."

"Excellent, until Friday then, my friend."

Raven rose out of her chair.

Reed remained seated.

"Yes, until Friday, my *friend*."

As Raven brushed past Reed, she reached down to cup Reed's right breast.

Before she could make contact, Reed grabbed Raven's hand and bent back her thumb.

Raven winced in pain, though she smiled bravely.

"Try that again, and I'll snap your wrist like a cheap chopstick," Reed said in a hushed voice.

She released Raven's hand.

"Oh well, thought it was worth a shot. Toodles."

Raven sashayed out of the Fountain Grille.

Wonder how the judges scored that round, Reed thought.

24

———————

Chance sat behind the wheel of his battleship class Denali SUV docked in the Safety Harbor Spa parking lot.

It was the kind of temperate and sunny winter day in Florida that drove New England chowder heads, corn-fed Hoosiers, and shoofly pie Pennsylvanians mad with envy.

As Chance listened to Richard Wagner's *The Ring of the Nibeling*, he sipped on black coffee from a 7-Eleven. He waved his arms vigorously as the Wagnerian composition approached its crescendo. He then spilt hot coffee on his lap.

He didn't flinch. Didn't swear.

Well, I'll be drawn and quartered, he thought.

Suddenly, Raven swung open the front passenger door.

She jumped into the Denali with the agility of a gymnast.

"Looks like you peed in your pants again, bubba," she said gleefully.

Chance gave Raven a Wile E. Coyote smile.

"I recognize that smile, Chance. If you can tell me what that 'E' stands for in Wile E. Coyote, I'll let you massage my feet."

This time, Chance smiled more broadly.

"Ethelbert."

"Very good. I knew you'd get it."

"How'd it go with Little Reed Riding Hood?"

Raven giggled as she put on her seatbelt.

"It went swimmingly, honey buns. Made her suspect I was drunk so she'd think my guard was down."

"What'd ya drink?"

"Three or four gin and tonics. Gave me a sweet little buzz, which helped me deal with her high and mighty attitude. She kinda pished me off."

"Pissed."

"Wha?"

"It's 'pissed'. You said 'pished'."

Raven giggle snorted.

"Raven, did you tip your cards with her?"

"Don't think so. Told her Megan was staying with us. Played dumb about Vlad. Have to give it to O'Hara. She wore a sarong thing showing off her boobies. Tried to distract me, just like I did to her at the Hangar. She's a smart one, and maybe as sneaky as I am."

Chance pulled out of the lot and headed south on Bayshore Boulevard, which was lined with neo-Med mansions hoisted on cement pylons, allowing the home owners to view the bay above the protected Mangroves lining the shore.

"She asked about Megan and Vlad, huh? Think she's on to us?"

Raven turned down Wagner.

"Sorry, but you play your music too loud and proudly. Yeah, O'Hara has her suspicions, looks like. But she was just getting her line wet today."

"Worried?"

"Ha. Not one bit."

Chance turned left onto the Tampa Causeway.

With the bay at a near dead calm, and against a broad background of almost cloudless blue sky, people skimmed across Tampa Bay on wave-runners and jet skis. Families grilled hot dogs, sausages, and burgers on the shoreline as the children and dogs splashed around in the water. A deputy sheriff sat in her cruiser, making certain no one consumed alcohol or drugs.

"Pretty out here, isn't it?" Chance said. "Thought you might enjoy the scenic route."

"Yes, real pretty, but I thought coloreds couldn't swim."

Husband and wife laughed together.

Raven absentmindedly chewed on a fingernail. She bit off a tiny piece of OPI "Show Me Your Tips" nail polish and spit it out of her mouth.

Chance shook his head and exhaled loudly.

"What?" Raven asked.

She began chewing on another nail.

"Just had the Denali washed, waxed, and vacuumed. Do you really need to do that? How about you spit it out the window?"

Raven waved off Chance dismissively.

"Whatever, I'll have Megan vacuum your precious truck when we get home."

"Well, all right then. Seriously, though, still going forward with your plan?"

Raven rubbed her right temple.

"Erm, so far, not a whole lot has gone right, except for my encounter with O'Hara on New Year's Eve and the lunch I just had with her. The kidnapping and Vlad escaping—talk about monumental screw-ups. Beginning to think I need to do everything myself."

Chance patted Raven's knee.

"No way, Jose. This is too big for one person, even for someone like my Dixie goddess."

Raven rubbed her left temple this time, saying "I'm a god, not a lame goddess."

She had taken off her ankle boots and sat cross legged.

"But you're right, Chance. It's just frustrating finding good people. You know, I told Jimmie to study those photographs we took of Andre. I think the little twit barely looked at them. Shoulda put Colt in charge."

"Probably shoulda, but it's easy to look back and find fault in your planning. Besides, Jimmie's done, and Colt's stepping up real nice, at least for as long as we need him."

Raven stopped chewing on her nails.

"Good thing Colt's stepping up. And I don't know about that Megan. She lets on it was an accident about Vlad. And I can't believe we haven't found that darkie yet."

Chance understood his wife was about to go off on a gin-fueled rant.

He exited Tampa Causeway and on-ramped the Veterans Expressway. They would arrive home within twenty minutes.

"Still gonna take out O'Hara?"

"Yes, with extreme prejudice. We can't have her undercutting our good work anymore. No more zero-sum game playing."

"Amen, sweetheart, amen. Friday still a go?"

"At Namaste? You know full well it is. You're just trying to get me to keep looking forward. And I appreciate that, my handsome hubby. Wouldn't know what I'd do without you."

Raven took Chance's gargantuan right hand and placed it on her left breast.

"Thank you for keeping me focused, Chance Doyle."

Though he kept his eyes on the road, he tenderly caressed Raven's breast.

"Oh, the pleasure's all mine, ma'am."

Chance pulled up to the iron gates at the equestrian estate.

He keyed in the security code and the gates parted ever so slowly.

"Think I'll put Megan on a leash and parade her around Namaste. Won't that just knock O'Hara off her game?"

Chance smiled.

"Good girl. You keep that wicked brain working."

25

———

"**J**ag älskar dig!"

In the middle of making love with Ravel, Sierra cried out in Swedish that she loved Ravel.

It was nine a.m. on Wednesday.

Sierra was a tall blonde beauty from Stockholm. She performed at Namaste and assisted Andre with security at the nightclub and she was terribly in love with Ravel, who insisted on a more friends-with-benefits arrangement.

Ravel smacked Sierra on her muscular left buttock.

"There will be no more of that, missy. You know our agreement—no mushy love talk during sex. What am I going to do with you?"

Sierra almost was a foot taller than her Swiss lover. She also had a good sixty pounds on her, and most of that was muscle and menace. She was highly intelligent, though not on Ravel's level, which wasn't unique, as Ravel considered Reed her only intellectual equal. Typical of relationships that paired a tiny partner with a much larger one, Ravel was the alpha; Sierra ceded that position as long as Ravel remained attracted to her.

Sierra stretched out on her back then said, "Feels like we've been playing Twister."

Ravel put her head on Sierra's shoulder and started to fall asleep.

"Not fair, Ravel, not fair at all."

Ravel opened her eyes.

"What now?"

"You know what, you imp."

Ravel reached over and made circles with her index finger on Sierra's stomach, slowly drawing in the circles until she reached her partner's navel. Sierra closed her eyes and smiled. Ravel repeated her circling. This time, she barely touched Sierra's skin.

"You know I can't be mad at you for long when you do that."

Ravel continued to circle Sierra's flat stomach.

"Relax those abs, you show off. Right now. And besides, why be mad at me? Remember what I called it, our Genevagina Agreement—no schoolgirl love gushing during sex. When it comes to love, I stay neutral. Let's enjoy this without using the 'L' word. We cross that line, and there's no going back. If we rush it, there's a fifty-fifty chance it will end poorly. Am I right or am I right? Now come on, let's snooze for a while."

Sierra ran her hand through Ravel's short black hair.

Then she grabbed a handful of the hair and yanked.

"Almost worked, Ravel."

"Ow! What *now*? Why can't we nap?"

Sierra held her grip on Ravel's hair and moved her small head from side to side.

"No, no, no. We're going to talk. Now."

Ravel made a grumpy face, then attempted to caress Sierra's breasts.

"Sure you want to talk, sweetie?"

Sierra pushed away Ravel's hand.

"Yes, I'm sure. Why can't you fall in love with me? I bring a lot to the dinner table."

Sierra let go of Ravel's hair.

Then Ravel giggled softly.

"'Table'. Not 'dinner table'. Just 'table'."

"Whatever, Ravel."

Whether a dinner table, a table of contents, or the periodic table of elements, Sierra brought much to any table.

She was five-feet, ten-inches of pure Scandinavian power and intellect.

She earned a bachelor's degree in biomedical engineering from the prestigious Lund University in Sweden. Infatuated with Florida—the balmy weather and the absence of annoying bull moose and arctic squirrel especially enticed her—Sierra attained a master's degree in general engineering at the University of South Florida in Tampa. Rather than return to Sweden, she decided to test the job market in Tampa Bay. Unfortunately, she found no employment as an engineer. Bouncing from one tedious office job to another, barely able to pay her bills and rent, Sierra decided to put to work one of her major assets: her intoxicating beauty that came with an alluring Swedish accent.

Tampa was awash with strip clubs, so she interviewed at several, settling on Babylon on Dale Mabry Highway. Babylon portrayed itself as an upscale strip joint. There was a dress code. Bouncers kept close watch on the dancers and the customers. With cameras everywhere, dancers didn't dare engage in prostitution—at least not on the property. Management, not the bouncers or dancers, controlled the surreptitious sale of cocaine and oxy.

An open-minded Swede, Sierra viewed this as a temporary solution for making money.

Benefiting from years of gymnastics and dance classes, Sierra took to the stripper pole with the enthusiasm of an NYPD firefighter on a midnight five-alarm call. With her long legs, sculpted body, and cascading blond hair, Sierra was an instant legend at Babylon, resulting in her amassing a six-figure income, most of it going unreported. Babylon's well-off clientele carpet bombed her with cash, jewelry, watches, and, curiously enough, box after box of shoes, which came exclusively from a foot-fetished Rack Room franchise owner. The more she turned down these men for "dates," the more gifts they gave her.

But trouble loomed.

Stripping was that rare vocation where employers actively encouraged alcohol consumption among the strippers, since customers drank more if dancers joined them, and they spent more money on expensive lap dances. Plus, a Red Bull with vodka emboldened a dancer on stage. Sierra found herself drinking more and more, and she began using cocaine. She sometimes felt ashamed of her work. She hardly could fly in her parents from Sweden to witness how she put her college degrees to work. Consequently, anesthetizing her guilt with alcohol and drugs became a necessity.

Openly gay, she couldn't maintain a serious relationship, since she suffered the stripper stigma and her late-night work schedule made dating nearly impossible.

Then one night, Ravel ambled into Babylon.

It was like at first sight.

After several private lap dances, Ravel was smitten with Sierra, who was strongly attracted to the little Swiss missy. Towards the end of the night, Sierra gave Ravel a modest kiss—a major protocol violation. She asked Ravel to wait for her once she got off work. Ravel quickly agreed.

And there was Ravel, standing in the Babylon parking lot at three-thirty in the morning, trying not to look over eager.

With a full moon illuminating the tropical night, Sierra walked up to Ravel and kissed her passionately.

Three nearby bouncers cheered.

After breakfast at Village Inn, the pair stayed the night at Sierra's condominium on Harbour Island. They spent the entire day making love, napping together, talking nonstop, and drinking one café latte after another. Surprisingly, Sierra didn't object to Ravel discovering the Swede's vial of cocaine and flushing the white powder down the toilet.

Late in the afternoon, Ravel brought up Namaste. She suggested Sierra visit the cabaret one evening, simply to get a feel for the place. If she were interested, she could dance at Namaste, as long as she swore off alcohol and illegal drugs.

Later that night, Sierra called in sick at Babylon and spent the evening at Namaste. The next day, Sierra interviewed with Reed, who summarily made a job offer to her. Sierra accepted.

She was even more successful at Namaste than at Babylon. Plus, there wasn't a stripper pole. Nor were there any lap dances or alcohol and drug abuse. Best of all, there were no grabby creepsters or love piners.

And Andre trained her to be his security assistant. At Reed's suggestion, Sierra earned a first-degree black belt in tae kwon do. Andre taught her the proper use of firearms, and helped her to obtain a concealed weapon permit. After multiple trips to the firing range, she became an excellent marksman. She even taught self-defense to her fellow performers.

However, despite all of these positive changes in her life, Sierra's love life remained complicated due to a major roadblock: Reed O'Hara. Though Ravel was completely in love with her, Reed could not and would not return that love.

Sierra held Ravel in her king-size bed.

"Ravel, you could try loving me while waiting for Reed."

Ravel shook her head then said, "Afraid it doesn't work that way, my delicious Swedish meatball. Try this out: I love Reed in the same way you love me. And we can love only one person at a time."

A tear rolled down Sierra's cheek.

"Am I a fool to hope you'll change your mind?"

Ravel wiped away the tear.

"Not a fool, just a fount of optimism."

The two women hugged ferociously.

Ravel broke away first.

"Come on, buck up, Sierra. We need to stratergerize here."

"About Raven Doyle?"

"Yuppers. Chenoa and I haven't found out anything about Vlad or Megan. Zip. Zero. Nada. We have talked with *everybody*. Our problem is neither of us knows too many white supremacists."

"Has Reed made any progress?"

"She had lunch with Raven over in Safety Harbor. Her intuition was spot on: Raven is definitely the bad guy in this sitch. And we know where Megan is—she's hanging out over at Raven's dude ranch. She apparently doesn't want to leave. Pardon the pun, cutie pie, but I'm worried Megan's come down with a nasty case of Stockholm Syndrome."

Sierra tsked.

"That is *such* a bad pun, but I get what you're saying. What does Reed think about Vlad's whereabouts?"

"She suspects that Vlad and Megan are Raven's captives. But we can't afford to waste time, so Reed wants me to check out that la dee da equestrian estate."

Sierra harrumphed.

"I am not doing the Jehovah's Witnesses bit again."

Ravel laughed.

"Yeah, that was a friggin' disaster. No worries, though. Reed has come up with a delightfully devious plan. She asked me and Sehar to go over there and pretend Sehar wants to jockey for Raven."

"Will Raven buy it?"

"Yes, because Sehar has the most honest face I've ever seen. She could tote a grenade launcher into an airport and still board a plane."

Sehar was a performer at Namaste. Reed and Jake hired her as a temporary replacement for the Ukrainian Tatiana, who was out on maternity leave. Sehar performed so well, she was given a permanent position once Tatiana returned.

Since Namaste was a cabaret-style nightclub, several of the women bared their breasts while performing. Sehar declined to show her breasts, which was entirely her option. Modesty was too important to Sehar, and it was because of Sehar Reed felt compelled to reconsider the bawdier element of Namaste performances. Yes, Reed reasoned, Moulin-Rouge featured bare-breasted dancers, but this was Tampa Bay, not Paris. Reed now felt certain she eliminated even the smallest connection to the plethora of strip joints surrounding Namaste.

Sehar came to Tampa Bay by way of Bombay, India. Hers was a conservative, wealthy family that honored all Hindu traditions, including arranged marriages. Sehar explained to Reed that she fled India because of an arranged marriage her family foisted upon her. Though that wasn't the entire story, since Sehar was gay. Her father, normally of a pleasant and sanguine personality, angrily threatened an honor killing if she did not renounce her forbidden sexuality and agree to the arranged marriage. A more tolerant and mettlesome uncle gave her the funds to escape from India.

Sehar chose Tampa Bay because its climate paralleled Bombay's and she believed there was ample opportunity to start a new life.

Lacking work experience, she found employment only at fast-food restaurants and convenience stores.

Sehar heard about Namaste from a friend.

Jake interviewed her and promptly offered a temporary position as a performer of the classical Indian dance of Kathak.

"What exactly is your mission at that horse farm?" Sierra asked.

Ravel drew circles again on Sierra's stomach.

"It's a two-parter—make contact with Megan, look for Vlad. Piece of cake."

"Does Sehar know how to ride horses?"

Ravel laughed.

"Sorry, but did you think Reed would send her out with no riding experience?"

"Ravel, don't be so mean."

"Sweetheart, sometimes you have to be cruel to be kind. Yes, Sehar grew up riding horses. Heck, you know her very well. She's maybe five-feet tall and weighs ninety pounds soaking wet. She was born to jockey a horse."

"When do you go over there?"

"Today. At three. I'll swing by and pick up Sehar, then we'll boot scoot boogey over to the *equestrian estate, dahling.*"

Sierra turned on her side to face Ravel.

Ravel gently cupped her full breast.

"That feels very nice," Sierra said.

She, in turn, ran her hand over the scars on Ravel's chest. Sierra was the only person allowed to touch Ravel's scars.

Maybe one day Reed will do that, Ravel thought as she closed her eyes and tilted her head back slightly.

"Min alskare, let me go with you and Sehar. We'll take my Jag, so there'll be room for the three of us."

Ravel appeared to ponder Sierra's idea.

"You're very persuasive right now, but Reed wants only me and Sehar to go."

"Isn't that just great! Why am I getting shut out?"

Ravel put her small, delicate hand on Sierra's left cheek.

"Because Reed has plans for you. For you and Andre more precisely."

Sierra's Baltic blue eyes lit up like a prayer candle.

"Really? Truly? Tell me now. Please."

"Can't say, because I don't know. Reed won't tell me. You know how she is, her plans have a lot of moving parts. The people involved get to know only the part of the plan we need to know."

"I see your point."

"Good. My guess is Reed doesn't want to tip her cards about you to Raven. Not just yet, at least."

"Makes sense but promise me you'll be careful."

"Of course I will, snookums. Now come on, let's snuggle and take a nap."

Ravel put her head on Sierra's shoulder.

She whispered into Sierra's ear, "And quit pulling my hair, woman."

With that, they drifted off to sleep.

26

———————

Driving her Porsche Boxster, Ravel swooshed into Providence Lakes in Brandon, a community fifteen miles east of Tampa. As usual, she was on time.

She pulled up to Sehar's well-kept ranch house, which was the color of blood oranges.

Though she leased the house, Sehar treated it as if it were her own. She herself mowed and edged the verdant Bahia lawn. Once a month, she trimmed the wax myrtle hedges in front of the house—after reading these hedges would swallow a home if left unattended in Florida's lush tropical environment. Sehar planted French marigolds everywhere, knowing the scent of the marigolds repelled mosquitos. She regularly pruned a drake elm tree that stretched its delicate boughs with feigned indifference in the center of the lawn.

Neighborhood looks kinda Stepford Wifey, Ravel thought.

She beeped her piercing car horn three times.

Two squirrels scampered up the drake elm.

Run, you furry tailed rats, she thought.

Sehar, dressed in a white tee shirt, blue denims, and tan riding boots, rushed out of her home and into the Boxster.

"Ravel, please do not blare your horn. I'll get reported to the Homeowner's Association. This community is deed restricted."

"*Humpf*, whatever that means."

"A deed-restricted community? It's where you agree to abide by certain rules and restrictions ... oh, never mind!"

Ravel laughed heartily.

"Gotcha, Sehar."

She launched her Porsche down the street with the aggressive vigor of Danica Patrick.

"Ravel! No speeding. Please. There are children at play as well as cats and dogs roaming around."

Ravel nodded, then down shifted to twenty miles per hour.

"Sorry, pumpkin. We have forty-one minutes to get to the horsey farm."

"The way you're driving, we'll be twenty minutes early."

Ravel put her hand on Sehar's knee.

"You are just so adorable."

Sehar pushed Ravel's hand away.

"That is most unprofessional and unwanted. *Really*, Ravel."

Ravel motored onto Interstate 75, heading north to Raven's equestrian estate in Northwest Hillsborough County.

She shifted silkily into sixth gear.

"I'm sorry, Sehar. You're right—that was unprofessional of me. Impulse control isn't my strong suit. I really do apologize."

Sehar *tsked*.

"Isn't Sierra your girlfriend?"

Ravel used the controls on her steering wheel to lower the volume on the deep house chill station.

"Yeah, I guess she's my girlfriend, but we aren't entirely exclusive. Always good to have a little flexibility, right?"

Sehar frowned at Ravel then turned her attention to a Confederate flag the size of Mississippi waving bombastically not three hundred feet from the Interstate. The flag was a genuine attention getter, causing many drivers to express disgust over the racist and traitorous symbol, while probably just as many drivers gave it a friendly Dixie rebel yell. Its sequoia-sized flagpole, however, was planted on private property, so there was no removing it any time soon.

"That flag is most disturbing," Sehar said. "It would be as if my parents in India put the Union Jack on their front lawn."

Ravel smiled.

"Did you know the Union Jack is a combination of the Scottish, Irish, and English flags?"

"Of course, I know that, you're simply trying to distract me from your inappropriate gesture."

Ravel smiled again.

"Guilty as charged."

"Listen to me, Ravel. I am being very serious now. I sense Sierra loves you, and it is you who wishes to keep her options open. So while you are with Sierra, I will not let you play paddle cakes with me. Do you understand?"

Ravel snort laughed.

"'*Paddle* cakes?' Too rich, just too darn rich. Okie dokie, Sehar of the Suwanee, no more – 'paddle cakes'—or even patty-cakes, for that matter. I will comport myself in a most proper manner. Deal?"

Sehar smiled.

"Deal."

As it turned out, thanks to Ravel's channeling her inner Danica, she and Sehar were twenty minutes early for their appointment with Raven and Chance Doyle.

The massive, forbidding iron gates to the horse farm opened automatically.

Impressive, Raven saw us pull up, Ravel thought.

She drove down a paved private road lined with magnificent magnolia trees adorned with dinner-plate-size white blooms that had arrived early. Ravel lowered the Boxster's windows so that she and Sehar might savor the sweet aromatic scent of the white magnolia blooms. A grey thoroughbred raced in a Kentucky blue grass pasture alongside the sports car. The horse's blonde mane and tail moved majestically with the beat of the horse's playful gallop.

"This is a most beautiful place," Sehar said happily.

"Yeah, well, there's trouble looming in paradise. Check out that dude."

A tall dark-haired man stood at an entrance to a service road. He wore a white cowboy hat, Armani sunglasses, a black tee shirt, black jeans, and tan cowboy boots.

"That's Chance Doyle," Ravel said. "Nice looking man. Reminds me of Jake, or at least Jake's dark side of the moon."

Chance waved Ravel into the service road and directed her to a large horse paddock and stables surrounded by white-rail horse fences —creosote fences fell out of favor when it was discovered the toxic black tar was unhealthy for horses and for humans as well.

A perfectly manicured horse track was near the stables.

Raven sat in a rickety chair in front of the barn entrance. She held a Mason jar of what appeared to be iced tea. A sprig of mint and a sterling silver straw flirted with one another in the Mason jar. Raven sat with her elbow tips on her knees. Her feigned indifference, so calculated and studied, would have made Sehar's drake elm Mean Joe Green with envy.

Doesn't fool me one bit, that's a cunning, dangerous woman, but wowzie woww wow she's cute, Ravel thought.

She and Sehar got out of the Porsche and walked toward Raven, who rose from her chair smiling.

Raven wore metallic-blue mirror Oakley sunglasses, a black sequined halter top blouse, torn blue jeans, and tiny cowboy boots.

Wow, Reed has a pair of boots just like those, Ravel thought.

That is a most attractive woman, she does not look at all scary, Sehar said to herself.

Looks like the three of us are having a midget convention, Raven thought.

"Hello, I'm Raven Doyle. How the heck are ya?"

"We are fine and dandy, Raven," Ravel said. "Sorry about being so early."

"No need to apologize to me, because if you're on time ...."

"You're late," Ravel interjected.

"Ha! I think I am going to like you."

Ravel shook hands with Raven.

Woman's got quite a grip, Ravel thought.

Those purple eyes look real, my oh my, what a tasty little tartlet, guvnor, Raven remarked to herself.

"Raven, I'm Brett, and this is my friend, Titli, your next jockey."

Raven giggled like a schoolgirl.

"'Titli', what an *unusual* name. Where's it from? Do folks call you 'Tit' for short?"

With her wheatish brown complexion, it was difficult to notice Sehar blushing wildly.

"Oh, no, Mrs. Doyle. 'Titli' is Hindi for 'butterfly'. I am from India, New Delhi, India."

Raven smiled impishly.

"Okay if I call you 'Dot'?"

Sehar giggled.

"I actually don't mind that nickname. It makes me laugh."

"Good girl, Titli. Keep an open mind about my bent sense of humor, and I'll try to be open minded about your not being from around these parts. Fair enough?"

"Fair enough, Mrs. Doyle."

"Call me Raven, Titli."

"Raven it is, then."

"So, I take it you're an experienced rider."

"Oh, yes, Mrs. ... Raven. My family in India owns several thorough-breds. My father taught me to ride competitively, and I've won many amateur competitions. Sadly, professional women jockeys are still nonexistent in India."

"Except for Rupa Singh, love. She's ridden over seven hundred winners."

"Yes, well, Rupa is the exception that goes to prove the rule, isn't she?"

Raven took a long pull of her iced tea through the sterling silver straw.

"Sorry, would y'all like some sweet tea?"

"No thank you, Raven," Sehar said.

"Oh God no," Ravel answered while shuddering.

Raven shrugged her shoulders.

"So is that why you came to America, to make a living riding on the back of a horse, Titli?"

"Exactly. I have only one skill: I can make a thoroughbred want to win."

Raven smiled at Sehar.

"I have to admit, it was funny your calling me out of the Blue Hawaii. But what the heck, let's see whatcha got."

Chance prepped a black thoroughbred for Sehar to ride.

A young woman with long auburn hair in a ponytail assisted Chance.

There's our Irish lass, Ravel thought.

Raven, Sehar, and Ravel walked over to the horse, who seemed accustomed to the attention.

Chance sized up Ravel and Sehar as if they were horse flesh.

Got no use for that brown girl, but the other one is a smoking hot tamale, Chance thought as he openly leered at Ravel.

Never in a million years, Ravel said to herself.

"Chance, here's Titli and ... I'm sorry, what's your name again?"

Ravel smirked at Raven.

"Brett. The name's Brett."

"Right. Thanks. Chance, this is Brett."

Chance tipped his white cowboy hat and flashed his diabolical smile.

"Pleased to meet you, ladies."

"Oh, and this is Megan, our most recent acquisition on the farm. She's been wonderful here."

Megan adjusted the horse's tack, while nodding to Ravel and Sehar.

Ravel gave what she hoped was a sly wink to Megan, who didn't let on she saw it.

Raven looked directly at Sehar.

"Here you go, Titli. Meet Monitor, seventeen hands of pure blood harmony and majesty."

Sehar reached into her jean pocket and pulled out a small carrot.

"May I, Raven?"

"Of course, start that bond early between horse and rider with a yummy treat."

Sehar stroked Monitor's long black face and whispered her introduction. She opened her small hand and Monitor lipped the carrot. One crunch and he was done, looking for more treats.

"Just like that, friends already," Raven observed.

"Beauty and the beast, right?" Ravel said to no one in particular.

Despite the pastoral overload, which was especially challenging for the card-carrying urbanite Ravel, she gradually grew more comfortable with the sights and sounds and smells of a horse farm. Her only concern was she might track horse dung into her Porsche.

Chance stood next to Ravel, his tall frame towering over her.

"Yeah, Monitor is a real beauty."

Ravel craned her neck to look up at Chance.

"What did you say, cowboy?"

Chance smiled mischievously.

This oughta be fun, he thought.

"Just messing with you, city girl."

Ravel gave Chance an alluring smile as counterfeit as the Coach tote knockoff slung over her left shoulder.

(At Reed's encouragement, Ravel agreed to leave behind her laptop, use a purse, wear a shirt with a collar, don clean jeans, and put on knotted macramé sneakers. She even agreed to apply make-up. The aim was to distract both Raven and Chance.)

"I like being messed with, actually," she said in an archly sexy voice.

Chance *harrumphed*.

"Then I'm the right man for the job, you garter-snapping Dixie pixie."

Impulse control, don't hit him, breathe, breathe, focus on the mission, Ravel thought.

"You, sir, are a silver-tongued devil. Does your wife ever let her horndog off the porch?"

Chance placed his hand on Ravel's left breast.

"All the time, baby."

Raven pretended not to notice Chance's sexual advance on Ravel.

"Hop on Monitor, Titli. He's all warmed up. My track is eight furlongs. Cost me a boatload of money. It's composite—polypropylene, recycled rubber, synthetic fibers, and sand. You and Monitor will love it. Saves his legs and your little brown behind."

Ravel pushed away Chance's hand.

"Eight furlongs?" she asked.

Raven didn't bother to look at Ravel when she answered her.

"Yup, eight furlongs equals one mile. Perfect length to test a horse's strength and willpower. C'mon now, Titli, time's a wasting. Let's do this!"

Sehar put on a black riding helmet and goggles.

Megan gave Sehar a jockey jump, holding one of her boots and hoisting her on the horse.

She sat confidently in the saddle.

"Stirrups okay?" Megan asked.

"They are perfect."

Sehar tightened the reins to let Monitor know she was in charge.

Megan offered her a riding crop.

"Goodness, no, I never use a whip. I respect and love horses too much to be so cruel."

Then she whispered briefly to Megan, *"Keep an eye on my friend if you want to leave here."*

Megan didn't react.

Chance guided Sehar and Monitor to the practice track. Monitor appeared impatient. His nostrils flared. He jerked his head at the reins. He was ready to do what he was born to do: gallop full out with wild lustful abandon. Sehar leaned forward and patted his neck.

"Easy, easy, baby. Won't be long before we take off."

It was a faintly cool winter afternoon. There was a slight breeze. No rain clouds in sight. The Florida sunshine even cooperated by sautéing rather than searing. In other words, it was an ideal day for Monitor to sprint a mile without generating too much of a lather.

Sehar trotted Monitor to the starting line.

Raven and Chance stood by the white-rail fence.

"And they're off!" Raven yelled.

Sehar gently kicked Monitor, who took off with the ferocity of a Shelby Cobra. Within two furlongs, Sehar had Monitor galloping at full speed. She rode parallel to Monitor, her stirrups high, her backside rhythmically rising and falling with each gallop.

Chance held a stopwatch.

"Look at that time! She doesn't need a whip, does she?"

"She's good, darn good," Raven said with admiration in her voice.

Staying in character, Ravel appeared so nervous about Sehar, she paced aimlessly in the paddock.

Raven and Chance paid her no mind, as they were too focused on Sehar and Monitor.

However, Megan watched Ravel. Very carefully and on the sly. Ravel got down on one knee to adjust a sneaker. She carefully pulled an object from her tote and slipped it into a dung heap. No one but Megan saw her do it. Ravel gave her a subtle nod, which Megan returned.

"Final stretch, Titli, final stretch!" Raven screamed, knowing the rider couldn't hear a word.

Sehar and Monitor stampeded across the finish line.

She slowed the heavy-breathing horse to a trot then to a walk, as they began the cool down lap around the track.

"Well?" Raven asked eagerly of Chance.

"One minute, thirty-two seconds."

"See, didn't I tell you he's an absolute stud," Raven exclaimed.

"Yes, ma'am, you did indeed. Course, give some credit to Titli."

"Hmm, maybe I will, maybe I won't," Raven responded petulantly.

Ravel approached Raven and Chance.

"Is that a good time? I know absolutely nothing about horse racing."

"It's a superb time, Brett," Raven said enthusiastically.

Raven suddenly hugged Ravel. As her hug lingered, she ran her right hand down Ravel's back, resting her hand on Ravel's derriere.

Great, getting tag-teamed by these two creeps, this is absolutely the last time I dress up, Ravel thought.

She deftly wiggled out of Raven's embrace.

"Sorry, Raven, but I'm in an exclusive."

"Figured you were, beautiful thing that you are. It was nice checking out your bum, though."

Sehar and Monitor approached the open track gate.

Megan held the reins as Sehar dismounted.

Colt led Monitor back to the paddock, where he would cool off the horse with a sudsy, relaxing bath.

Raven walked up to Sehar.

"Titli, you're one heck of a rider. Among the best I've seen. Your instincts are superb, and you let Monitor know you were the boss without abusing him. You have all the makings of an excellent jockey. Rotten shame I can't use you."

Sehar took off her helmet and goggles. Her tee shirt was soaked through with perspiration. She seemed ready to explode like a Guatemalan volcano.

"Why can't you use me? Was I not good enough?"

Chance stepped forward.

"You're plenty good. And I don't give out compliments very often. But there's a problem, and it's majorly big: you won't blend in very well around here."

Sehar stomped her riding boot.

"Because I am Indian?"

"Nope. Because you ain't white," Chance said with casual belligerence.

"Then why did you have me come here and ride Monitor? I do not understand. I left everything on that track. Everything."

Raven had her arms folded as she tapped her boot.

"There's not a whole lot to understand. I simply wanted to see what kind of rider Reed O'Hara would send me, *Sehar*."

Everyone stood in an uncomfortable silence.

Only the cicadas chattered away, Greek chorus style.

Raven motioned for Megan to give her a riding crop.

"You're sure, Megan?"

"Yes, ma'am."

Raven snapped the riding crop against her leg.

"Y'all just hold on," she said in a commanding tone.

She marched over to the dung pile in the paddock. After digging through the dung with the riding crop, she pulled out a phone. She didn't bother wiping it off.

Raven marched back to the group.

She looked at Megan.

"Good job, sweetie. Appreciate the heads up. You've restored my faith in you."

Megan smiled proudly.

"Thank you, Raven. Anything for the Cause."

Raven laser beamed Ravel.

"You must have dropped this phone in the horse dung, *Ravel*."

Then she called out to Colt, who emerged from the stable carrying a Remington 12-gauge pump shotgun.

"Whenever you're ready, Colt," Raven said in a motherly tone.

Colt went into shooting stance and raised the shotgun.

"Pull!"

Raven threw the phone high up in the air.

Colt tracked the phone, then blasted it into too many pieces to count.

Raven clapped.

"Good job, young man. Now go back in the stable and calm my babies and finish up with Monitor."

"Yes'm, right away."

Raven glared at Ravel.

"And the Raven, never flitting, still is sitting, *still* is sitting ... And my soul from out that shadow that lies floating on the floor shall be lifted—nevermore."

Ravel shook her head,

"Lady, you are bat guano crazy."

Red rage swallowed up Raven, making it appear she was about to re-enact the murders in the Rue Morgue.

"Get off my property before I have Colt use you for clay pigeons."

Unfazed by Raven's threat, Ravel simply extended her middle finger to her.

"Yes, most certainly I second what she did," Sehar said defiantly to Raven.

The women got into the Boxster.

As she started up her sports car, Ravel winked at Sehar.

"Why'd you wink at me?"

Ravel laughed loudly.

"Because, dahling, Raven found only one phone."

27

———————

I t was nine p.m. the same Wednesday.

Though most nightclubs did little business on Hump Day, Namaste stood out, as the nightclub almost always was at full capacity.

There were over two hundred guests in attendance that night. Andre had turned away at least a dozen couples.

One of the reasons for the nightclub's success was Nama-Stay, Jake's brainchild for bringing couples from around the world to immerse themselves in the tropical paradise that is Tampa Bay. Couples came from Hong Kong, Paris, Istanbul, Sydney, London, Tokyo, and Rome. Jake put them up at the Floridan Palace Hotel, the Vinoy, and the Don Cesar Hotel. For three days, the couples enjoyed treatments at the Safety Harbor Spa, played tennis and swam at Saddlebrook, and shopping spreed at Wiregrass, International Plaza, and St. Armand's Circle, or if they preferred, the upscale outlet malls north or south of Tampa Bay. The couples enjoyed long walks at Clearwater Beach and St. Pete Beach, and charter fished far out into the Gulf of Mexico.

During their excursions, Sierra, carrying a police baton and a Sig Sauer M11-A1 compact handgun, was on security detail for these couples, as not everyone in Tampa Bay welcomed obviously foreign tourists.

Each evening, the couples came to Namaste for dinner and a show. On this particular Wednesday night, there were three couples from Istanbul. The six of them were close friends. As return guests, they were proof positive Jake's Nama-Stay program was a keeper.

Normally, Jake oversaw nightclub operations and occasionally played piano—sometimes performing his own compositions—to accompany the performers' dance routines. But tonight was different: Jake felt it in his bones that Raven Doyle would make a move on Namaste, probably this week. So he shared security watch with Andre.

Jake stood at the bar while sipping on Perrier.

Andre approached him.

"Find out anything about Vlad?"

"Not really, though Ravel and Chenoa have been searching everywhere. No luck. The Doyles outed Sehar and Ravel at the horse farm. Looks as if Raven did her homework on us. At least Sehar and Ravel made contact with Megan, who appears to be doing okay. In fact, she could be coming around to our side. She told Raven about only one of two phones Ravel hid at the farm. As far as Vlad, they didn't see him there, although that wasn't likely anyway. I'm sorry, Andre."

Andre took a deep breath and exhaled slowly.

He put his hands on the bar and lowered his head.

"My baby brother. What a horrible nightmare. And it's all my fault."

"Cut that out, Andre. Right now. It's not your fault at all. It was a case of mistaken identity. These mooks were going after you, and they screwed it up royally. Crappy luck is all this is, okay?"

Andre raised his head and stood with broad shoulders squared. After all, like Jake and Reed, he was a professional who had a job to do.

"Yeah, you're right. Just wish those punks would've jumped me instead."

"Of course you do. But they didn't. They got Vlad. Those are the parameters in which we work, right? Do not give up hope; until we know differently, we commit that Vlad's alive. He's capable of dealing with his predicament. And he has some equally capable people looking for him. So we need to do our job by being alert and vigilant in protecting everyone at Namaste."

"Amen, Jake."

The two men were consummate professionals. They understood that other team members, other fellow professionals, were scouring Tampa Bay for any tip on Vlad's whereabouts. Jake and Andre's task, as delineated by Reed, was to keep Namaste running smoothly while protecting the guests, the performers, Chef Glenn and his staff, as well as the hosts, servers, bartenders, and especially the West African DJ, Koala.

Both men were ready to confront any problem at the nightclub.

Andre wore a long-sleeve black turtleneck shirt, black slacks, a charcoal gray sport coat, and black low-top sneakers. His Desert Eagle, more cannon than pistol, was holstered beneath his sport coat.

Jake's outfit was less formal than usual: a beige linen shirt, matching linen pants, and brown Mephisto sandals, the type of outfit allowing him to engage unrestrained in martial combat, should the need arise.

"Andre, when this is done, when Vlad and Megan return home safe and sound, when Raven and Chance Doyle are brought to justice, let's fly to Paris—you, Chenoa, Reed, and me—and stay for a week. We'll have croque monsieur at La Petit Wagram, lose our minds over the Impressionist paintings at the Musee d'Orsay, sip on café au lait at Cafe George V on the Champs–Élysées."

Andre nodded his approval.

"Oui, mon homme. That sounds wonderful. I hope Chenoa will join us."

"Oh, I'm certain she'll come. After all, with her passion for fashion, she won't miss a chance to shop at Galeries Lafayette."

"True that, but maybe she'll be motivated by more than shopping."

Jake smiled warmly at his colleague.

"She will, Andre. Je le garantis."

Right at that moment, the house lights went down, except for the stage.

Everyone stopped talking.

It was show time at Namaste.

Reed's aim in opening Namaste was to create a nightclub that face slapped the sleazy strip clubs popping up in Tampa Bay like so many toxic fungi spores.

A majority of the women who performed at Namaste had engaged in stripping and prostitution. Be it alcohol or tobacco or illegal drugs, these women were hardcore substance abusers. Some were flat-out addicts. Many of them were victims of parental and domestic abuse; not surprisingly, virtually all of them dropped out of high school. The women battled sexually transmitted diseases and complications related to being HIV positive. Theirs was a story told too often, and usually ended tragically.

Reed actively sought out these women, offering them safe harbor while they overcame their addictions and tried to lead healthy, productive lives once again.

And one of Reed's great success stories was about to take the stage.

Candace, like so many other Midwesterners, migrated from Wisconsin to Tampa Bay with the dream of a bright new start in her young life.

She grew up in Green Bay. Her parents were loving and generous, though she cared less and less for their many home rules. She excelled in high school, both in the classroom and on the soccer pitch. Occasionally, she was reprimanded for smoking a cigarette or fighting with a bully. When she arrived in Madison to begin nursing studies at the University of Wisconsin, she brimmed with optimism and confidence.

But it was while she was a Wisconsin Badger that Candace became known as "Candy".

Her college experience started out well. She attended every class and studied diligently. She attended Big Ten football games, sneaking in seven-ounce bottles of Stroh's beer while staying away from hard liquor. And she fell out of love as effortlessly as she fell in love. It felt good to be a frosh.

Then one November night in her dormitory, the cultural petri dish of college experimentation, a blizzard buffeted the campus with blinding snow and howling winds. In an attempt to escape the Wisconsin winter blues, Candace tried MDMA. Methylenedioxymethamphetamine. Molly. M&M. Ecstasy.

In a span of thirty minutes, Candace transformed into Candy.

With her senses heightened, she felt the psychedelic molecules swirling inside her. Her energy level rocketed to Pluto. The psychotropic chemicals surging through her produced sexual arousal she never had experienced.

Candace began dancing to Tom Petty and the Heartbreakers. Damning the torpedoes, she rocked and rolled with boys, with girls, with just herself. Perspiring heavily, Candace doffed her clothes. She danced completely naked while bathed in a purple and white strobe light. Someone called her "Candy" as she swayed erotically with a grape Tootsie Pop in her mouth.

(Just two weeks later, a lecherous English professor called her "Candy" during a discussion of Nabokov's *Lolita*. She was too stoned to object.)

Candy got hooked on ecstasy, but not in the sense of a physical addiction. She discovered a brave new world free from all social restraints. Candy spent more and more time going to underground raves, and less and less time going to class.

She lost control of her life.

Instead of trying to help her, her more conservative friends shunned her, while her more libertine friends encouraged her to party into the night.

Since she stopped attending class, Candy decided to sell her textbooks at the campus bookstore. She got pennies on the dollar for them, but at least she had cash to purchase more ecstasy, cigarettes, and cheapish vodka.

By the time Christmas break rolled around, Candy dropped out of the University of Wisconsin, returning home to Green Bay a drug dependent woman rife with guilt and STDs. She was completely defeated.

When she heard liquor distributors in Tampa hired attractive young women to promote their distilled spirits, Candy headed due Deep South. And right into a tropical depression of her own making. For no matter where Candy went, there she was, along with her bad habits.

The liquor distributors weren't interested in her. No legitimate business would hire an obviously drug-addled individual. It wasn't long before she was an escort to car salesmen, personal injury lawyers, and Shriners with shiners. She despised this work as well as herself, so she self-medicated with molly, cocaine, oxycodone, cigarettes, and Grey Goose Vodka.

Her brunette hair, once so long and lovely, was unkempt and cropped short. Those beautiful blue eyes were constantly bloodshot. Her skin bore the pallor of a George A. Romero zombie. A previously fit figure became waifish thin.

Candy was in need of sublime intervention.

Then one early morning, in the Constant Grind Cafe at the Tampa Hard Rock Hotel and Casino, she encountered Ravel, who sat alone, nursing a large cappuccino and staring at her laptop.

Candy got a black coffee then tentatively approached Ravel's table. She had had an especially rough night with a pair of pervy plumbers from Poughkeepsie.

"This place is slammed, mind if I join you?" Candy asked pleadingly.

Ravel didn't bother to look up.

"Hey, it's still a freak country. Go ahead. Pop a squat. But you start telling me some sad-sack story, all you'll get from me is, not my monkey, not my circus, not my problem."

Turns out, Candy did share her tough-luck story with Ravel, who listened with genuine interest.

That was because Ravel was out running point for Reed; her assignment was to look for distressed women who might shine to Reed's rehab program.

Candy cried over what Reed offered her: drug dependency treatment; freedom from alcohol and tobacco use; a return to nursing studies in the LPN program at Hillsborough Community College; exercise programs and dance classes; and all the while earning an honest living as a Namaste performer.

In time, as she progressed with her rehab, Candy returned to being called Candace.

"Ladies and gentlemen, our first performance of the night will be by our marvelous Maiden of the Midwest, Candace!" DJ Koala announced enthusiastically.

A single spotlight focused on Candace, who stood center stage, her head bowed, hands clasped in front of her.

Barefoot, she wore a white Panama straw hat, a tailored white linen suit, a lace blouse, and long pearl strands. Her intention was to evoke the character Jordan Baker, Daisy Buchanan's androgynous friend from F. Scott Fitzgerald's novel, *The Great Gatsby*.

Candace lifted her head and smiled warmly at the audience as they greeted her with applause. The three couples from Istanbul politely called out to Candace as they clapped wildly. She took off her hat and Frisbee'd it to the Turkish couples. One of the women, whose smooth brown skin was the color of a Turkish fig, caught the hat and popped it on her head.

Candace's shimmering brunette hair was bobbed. Her makeup mirrored the Flapper look from a century ago: heavy blush on the apples of her cheeks; dark red lipstick; long thin eyebrows; smoky eye shadow; curled eyelashes; and thick eyeliner that showcased her topaz blue eyes.

Candace was ready, so she signaled to DJ Koala to play "Crazy Rhythm" by Jazz Age Belgian guitarist Django Reinhardt.

In this song, Reinhardt combined his guitar play with trombones, saxophones, and trumpets to create a thirty-two-beat raging locomotive flying off the tracks.

> *Crazy rhythm, here's the doorway*
> *I'll go my way, you'll go your way*
> *Crazy rhythm, from now on, we're through*

Even though Reinhardt, on stage and in his personal life, couldn't escape the allure of the crazy rhythm lifestyle, Candace took the song to heart, as she embarked on a new life.

She joyfully dove into the Foxtrot, deftly moving across the stage to the frenetic beat of "Crazy Rhythm".

The audience cheered her on, and no more so than the three couples from Istanbul.

But a dark cloud loomed.

At a nearby table, a man and woman, both young and white, appeared upset with the Turkish party.

Though they didn't say anything, the man and woman scowled at the Turks, who did their best to ignore them, particularly since Candace had switched to performing the lively Toddle.

> *Here is where we have a showdown*
> *I'm too high and you're too lowdown*
> *Crazy rhythm, here's goodbye to you*

Candace then sailed gracefully into the Lindy Hop, and when she was about to take on the Black Bottom, the man and the woman pushed back their chairs as they stood up. Their attire certainly tested the nightclub's dress code: they both wore tee shirts, jeans, and cowboy boots. They appeared intoxicated and crazy angry.

"Don't be staring so greedy like at that white woman, ya brown mudders," the man yelled.

The Turks barely had time to react when the young woman poured her beer on one of the women.

The woman screamed in horror.

Her husband jumped out of his chair and charged at the man and woman.

Fortunately, Andre and Jake interceded before a brawl broke out.

Andre motioned for DJ Koala to cut the music and for Candace to exit the stage.

Jake gently, but firmly, held back the husband.

"This is most upsetting, Jake," Mr. Yildirum said. "My wife has been accosted with beer and her dress is ruined. And what does that mean, a 'brown mother'?"

The man and woman broke out in raucous laughter.

"Brown *mudder*, you mo-ron," the man said derisively.

Jake pointed at him.

"Shut your pie hole."

The young man smiled defiantly at Jake.

"No prob, gramps. But these dots were disrespecting that fine white lady dancer by oogie, boogling her."

"We most certainly did not disrespect her," Mr. Yildirum exclaimed. "And we are Turkish, not Indian, sir."

Mrs. Yildirum continued to cry and whimper.

"Time for you to hit the road, junior," Jake said with an authority that brooked no discussion.

The young man grabbed his crotch.

"Hey, that's cool. I think we got our point across, Jake Dupree."

The man and woman strode through the nightclub. They held up their chins and mock marched between the tables.

"White power, y'all," the woman screamed.

Andre followed behind them.

He carried in his left hand a retracted ASP security baton.

"Mr. Yildirum, I apologize for this incident." Jake said.

Mr. Yildirum patted his wife's shoulder.

"This was most unprofessional, Jake. Most unprofessional. You were supposed to protect us. You failed."

"Yes, I did fail, sir. I am deeply sorry for our breakdown in security. We should have anticipated this situation, then taken appropriate action. Of course, we will refund all of your Nama-Stay fees."

Mr. Yildirum's posture stiffened.

"I think you Americans use the expression, you add an insult to an injury. We refuse any refund at all. Except for this last night, you held up your side of the contract, we held up our side by paying you in full."

"Sir, what can I do to make amends?"

"Just return us safely to our hotel and make certain we arrive at the airport in the morning at least three hours in advance of our flight home to Istanbul."

"Done and done, sir."

"Do not think we will ignore this ugliness. I will instruct my dear wife to inform, in complete detail, all of the international luxury travel sites."

"That's fair, sir."

The two men shook hands then the three Turkish couples left Namaste.

Andre approached Jake.

"Lil' Abner and Daisy Mae Yokum are off the property."

"Good job, Andre. Once our guests are back at the Vinoy, see that our drivers stick around for a couple hours. And have Sierra accompany them. They don't need any more hassles."

"Will do, Jake."

Barry the bartender gave Jake and Andre iced glasses of Perrier.

"What do you make of tonight, Jake?" Andre asked.

Jake gave him a Lee Marvin smile, which was more grimace than grin.

"Raven Doyle gave us a broadside tonight. We're listing some, but still afloat, my friend. Let's buy everybody a round and have Candace perform again. Sorry, but I have to say it, the show must go on."

28

———————

Sitting on the veranda of their equestrian estate at eleven a.m. on Thursday, Raven and Chance finished an early lunch of cheeseburgers, fries, and watermelon.

Raven put her sandaled feet on Chance's lap.

"Please massage my feet, love. It helps me think."

"With pleasure, my beautiful Raven."

Chance removed her sandals and placed them under his chair. Raven dug her heels into his crotch. He began massaging her tiny feet with hands the size of jai alai cestas.

"*Oooo*, that's it, Chance. Feels *sooo* good."

"Cool. You know I live to serve my ravenous Raven, right?"

"Heh. You're so darn cute. And hey, where are those two idiots?"

Chance looked up from his handiwork.

"Arriving right about now, hon."

The couple booted out of Namaste the previous night ambled up to Raven and Chance.

"Morning, y'all," the young man said in a neighborly tone.

"You're late, Colt and Sissy," Raven said in a less than neighborly tone.

Sissy lowered her head. She was maybe an inch taller than Raven, had long sunflower blonde hair, and sported curves that'd dizzy even a NASCAR driver.

"We're so sorry, ma'am. Got a late start this morning. Colt has his manly needs, you know."

She giggled as she put her tiny doll hand over her mouth.

Colt shifted from one booted foot to the other, like some delinquent third grader facing old timey Principal "Hickory Rod" Stickler.

"Ma'am, we're really sorry for being late. It's all my fault, not Sissy's."

Chance winked at Raven, who winked back at her husband.

"I accept your apology, young man," Raven said with a judicious air. "I like your being a Southern gentleman—you took full responsibility for the both of you being late."

Colt took off his Dallas Cowboys trucker hat and put it on his chest.

"Thank you for your understanding, ma'am. Won't happen again. Promise."

Happens again, I could be a dead man, Colt thought.

"See that it don't, *boy*." Chance said in a pea-gravel voice.

"Yes, sir," Colt said quickly.

"You just remember who's the cock of the walk here," Chance said.

Humph, Raven, for sure, Colt thought.

"Yes, sir, I'll remember that you're the cock of the walk."

"Well, all right then."

Raven waved the couple to sit down.

"Give us a report on last night and leave nothing out."

"Devil's in the details, right, ma'am?" Colt said.

Raven flashed irritation at him.

"Whatever, just set your butt down and start talking."

Colt and Sissy sat down.

"Well?" Raven asked impatiently.

Colt cleared his throat.

"Yes, ma'am, um, we did like we was told: just went on in to that Namaste, got a table next to a bunch of mudders, and pretended to be buzzed."

"Then what?" Chance demanded.

Sissy spoke up.

She'd recently turned twenty-one. She was in love with the slightly older Colt, who got her involved with Raven and Chance, though she seemed more interested in the Colt than in the Cause.

"Sir, ma'am, we followed orders. No diver, uh, deviation whatsoever, just how you wanted. Like you told me, I went potty after twenty minutes."

Chance fingered his thick black mustache.

Man's got a ferret for a 'stache, Colt thought.

"Jake and Andre eyeball you?" Raven asked.

"Yes, ma'am, a little. We kinda stood out in that crowd," Colt said.

Sissy interjected, "We shoulda dressed nicer, me in a dress, Colt in a sports jacket. He wouldn't hear of it, but at least he left that stupid Cowboys lid at home."

"What the heck, Sissy? Why'd you bust on me like that?"

Sissy's eyes narrowed.

"You shoulda listened to me, is all. Besides, the Doyles want all of the details. Isn't that right, Mr. Doyle?"

"You bet, cutie pie," Chance replied.

He looked Sissy up one side and down the other, noting her ample physical attributes.

Not bad at all, can't believe I didn't spot those curves before, he thought.

He continued to leer at Sissy, who didn't seem to mind the attention. Colt started to object, but Sissy patted his knee and shook her head no at him. Chance smiled at Colt, as if he were daring the young man to challenge him.

"All right, move on, what happened next?" Raven asked.

Colt blinked a few times, trying hard to control his temper over Chance ogling Sissy.

"Ma'am, we gave those mudders the genuine stink eye for staring all creeper like at that fine white lady on the stage. Mudders ignored us for a while, but we kept at it. Like to be burning holes in 'em with our Taser laser stare. They got uncomfortable, started fidgeting in their chairs like a long-haul trucker 'bout ready to piss his pants."

Raven ran an index finger up and down her ski-slope of a nose.

Looks like she's picking her nose, Colt silently noted.

"Jake and Andre start to pay more attention?" Raven asked.

"A little, but it was a big room, with a lot of people," Sissy answered.

Chance winked at her.

Sissy smiled at him.

Raven slapped Chance's shoulder.

"Cut it out."

Chance grinned at her as he replied, "Sure, whatever you say, honey. I'll take a shot at behaving myself."

Raven shook her head in disgust.

"Then what'd you do, Colt?"

"I jumped up and I told those mudders to stop that eyeballing."

"Then I poured a beer on a mudder's wife," Sissy said excitedly.

Chance continued to stare at Sissy, who started to get annoyed. Sort of. Maybe.

"Y'all get a fight going?"

"Almost, sir," Colt said. "But Jake and his pet gorilla stopped it, then they threw us out."

Raven folded her hands on her lap.

"Y'all did a darn good job."

"Thank you, ma'am," Colt and Sissy said in unison.

Chance leaned forward in his chair.

"Time for you two to get a move on."

Not having to be told twice, Colt and Sissy practically leapt out of their chairs and power walked to the front of the mansion.

About twenty feet away, the couple stopped suddenly.

"I don't care, Colt, I am going to talk to that man and give him a righteous what for," Sissy said loudly.

"Don't, Sissy, you'll just mess things up," Colt pleaded.

"Nope, nope, nope. He ain't allowed to treat me like that. You stay here, I'll take care of this."

Colt stayed put; Sissy marched with determination back to Raven and Chance.

"This has possibilities," Chance said quietly.

"Nothing like a little fem drama to spice up the day, Chance dear," Raven added.

Sissy stood up straight, her shoulders squared. Curiously, she stood extremely close to the table, almost touching it.

"Ma'am. Sir. Sorry to bother you but I have to speak up."

"What's on your mind?" Raven asked.

Sissy paused then smiled radiantly with her back to Colt.

"Y'all like to have a threesome with me, give me a call," she said in a near whisper.

She slyly placed a piece of pink paper next to Chance's place setting.

"Those are my digits. Guarantee it, I'll make y'all forget about that Megan girl."

Obviously taken aback by her indecent proposal, Chance first had to clear his throat before responding.

"Erm, that's an attractive idea, Sissy. But Raven'll have to approve it before we can move forward—and backward."

This time, Sissy winked at Chance, then she looked over to Raven. "Ma'am?"

Raven gave her a teeny thumbs up.

"Yay, I'll get out of your hair, for now at least."

She rejoined Colt and the pair left the estate.

Chance picked up the pink paper and flicked it with his thumb.

"Well whatta you know. I still got it."

Raven smirked.

"Feeling all cocky right now, aren't you?"

Chance gave her a sexy grin.

"Maybe a little, but you get first crack at her."

Raven snorted.

"Of course I do. Hmm, I think the Lord is watching over us. Just when we're about to get rid of Megan, our little earth angel shows up. The Savior sure works in mysterious and wonderful ways."

"Amen."

"Now, let's go over again our plan for Friday night," Raven said in a commanding tone.

29

Chenoa laid her head on Andre's shoulder, their bodies still glistening from love making.

It was two p.m. on Thursday.

Andre worked late at Namaste. He arrived at Chenoa's condominium in West Chase well past four a.m.

Chenoa also had a late night, as she and Ravel scoured Hillsborough County in search of Vlad. They were not successful. Chenoa, however, succeeded in exhausting herself.

But not Ravel—the later it got, the perkier she became.

"What are you, Ravel, some kind of vampire, "Chenoa asked.

Ravel grinned like Puck in *A Midsummer Night's Dream*.

"Maybe I am."

Chenoa snuggled with Andre. She let out a long, satisfied breath.

She was almost six-feet tall and quite thin. Since she avoided being out in full sun and she never sunbathed, Chenoa had no tan lines, a wise move for a redhead with alabaster skin. Her magnificent mane of curly red hair stretched down her back.

Andre put his muscular arm around Chenoa.

His skin shone like a French Polynesian black pearl.

He was six-feet, five-inches tall and a chiseled two hundred fifty pounds.

"Chenoa, I think I'm falling for you."

She smiled dreamily.

"You'd better be, my Adonis."

They kissed passionately.

Andre held her face in his hands.

"Doing all right, milady?"

Chenoa giggled, slightly.

"You better believe it."

Andre became serious.

"Are we going anywhere with this, Chen?"

Andre and Chenoa became attracted to one another in a series of subtle stages. A sly smile from her. A playful wink from him. Professional conversations going on longer than usual. A slight touch of Chenoa's hand. An admiring gaze from her.

Certainly, the pair was conflicted. Andre's job: deliver near-complete protection of everyone at Namaste. Chenoa's job: assist Reed with private investigations, and always be available. Because of Namaste's non-fraternization rule, Chenoa approached Reed for an exemption. Reed at first was hesitant to grant another exemption, as she already had green-lighted Ravel and Sierra's relationship. In the end, though, she allowed it, not wanting to lose either Chenoa or Andre, who remained entirely professional while on the job.

"Yes, Andre, I think we are going somewhere with this ... relationship."

Chenoa kissed him lightly on his onyx cheek.

"Let's just take it slow, okay? I didn't date much before I became a nun. You know, of course, about my fling with Father Jack. But that was just what it was—a fling. I'm not experienced at all with long-term relationships with men."

Andre smiled dreamily.

"We'll take it as slow as you want, my dear."

Chenoa patted his shoulder.

"How are you holding up?"

Andre started tearing up.

Chenoa continued to pat his shoulder.

"Keep the faith, boo. I truly believe he is alive. We will find him."

Andre closed his eyes; a single tear cascaded down his cheek.

"I can't believe I'm having this wonderful time with you, and all the while my brother is missing. I feel so guilty."

"That's understandable. But you have Reed's orders to protect Namaste. All of us have our individual missions in finding Vlad. I believe in Reed, in her intelligence and savvy. You should as well, Andre."

He held Chenoa's chin.

"I will always have faith in Reed, but do you think we'll find Vlad alive?"

"I just know it, hon."

Andre kissed her.

"Hey, enough of this moping. Does nothing for my macho-man rating. I hope you know I love you very much."

Chenoa positively beamed.

"You make me so happy, Andre. I love you, too."

"Truly, with all of your heart?"

Chenoa gently pinched his right nipple.

"Of course, you goose."

Andre let out a booming laugh.

"Been awhile since I've felt this good. Won't be easy, but I have to learn to trust all of this."

"You'll get there. Remember, trust is the thing *without* feathers."

Andre laughed again.

"So trust is as naked as we are?"

Chenoa giggled.

"Yes, as naked *and* strong as we are. You only have to believe in it. It's a leap of faith that goes way beyond any religion or philosophy."

Andre kissed her again, as he cupped her creamy white breast.

Then he laid back.

"I need to talk with you about Reed's plan, at least the part that involves me. I'm not supposed to discuss it but you need to know, so you don't think I am fooling around."

Chenoa turned on her side and faced Andre.

She propped her head on her right elbow.

"I'm all ears, Andre."

"It requires me and Sierra working together, so please don't get jealous."

"I won't get jealous as long as you stay all mine."

"Fair enough, baby."

"Besides, jealousy is horrible for a person. It's the thing with fangs and claws."

"Yikes."

Andre then laid out in detail Reed's plan for him and Sierra. Chenoa listened intently, nodding several times as he spoke.

"Brilliant, simply brilliant, Andre."

"I think so, too. So, you're okay with me and Sierra?"

"Yes, absolutely."

"Thank goodness. Now here's something really interesting. Reed has never done this before. It's a true break with protocol. Normally, she tells each of us about individual tasks. We do not know what the rest of the team is doing. That way, we concentrate solely on what we have to do."

"So please tell me how this time is different."

"Reed appreciates I'm worried sick about my brother. She told me the overall plan's goal was twofold: put Raven and Chance behind bars and bring home Vlad and Megan. She said Ravel was instrumental in providing her key information. She believes tomorrow night may end happily for all of us."

"Oh, Andre, I'm so happy for you. There are no guarantees here, but I'm glad we have Reed on our side."

"And I'm glad I have you on my side as well, Chenoa. Listen, I have to leave in a bit to meet up with Sierra at Namaste."

Chenoa sat up.

"In that case, let's make love one more time."

Andre feigned exhaustion.

He couldn't help but marvel at her voracious sexual appetite, an obvious result of her forsaking vows as a nun.

Sure not going to complain, he thought.

He smiled broadly.

"Well, if you insist, love."

"Oh I do, Andre, I do."

30

R eed sat in lotus position in the exercise room of their penthouse.

It was Friday, nine a.m.

Jake got home late, as late as Andre the night before, and he managed about three fingers of sleep. Jake knew tonight would be complex and dangerous. He was reminded of the prep work he did for the assassinations he performed on behalf of the CIA. Lay the proper groundwork, prepare for the worst, and it still could be an utter cluster bust, Jake thought as he readied himself for the big showdown at Namaste.

Jake stepped in to the exercise room, gave Reed a freshly prepared cappuccino, then said, "I really should go to Namaste, Reed. Will you be okay?"

"Of course, I will, love. I cleaned my Glock last night, and I'll keep it by my side at all times. Please don't worry about me. Remember, I'm from West (By God) Virginia."

Jake kissed Reed, then left.

She thought of Andre, of how difficult this was for him, which is why she tipped her cards some to him.

She thought of her sister Debbie, who was only a year older than she.

Debbie lived in nearby St. Petersburg, affectionately known to locals as the 'Burg.

Sometimes, the two sisters got together to attend a concert at Ruth Eckerd Hall in Clearwater or the Mahaffey Theater in the 'Burg.

They tried to stay in contact, though it was difficult in light of Reed's busy life and Debbie's obligations as an executive with a bay area cable company.

The sisters were born into the Appalachian lifestyle and mindset of West Virginia, where it wasn't that long ago when the Ku Klux Klan lynched Black men on the South Side Bridge in Charleston.

Though their father was an avowed racist, Reed and Debbie were brilliant and open-minded souls who fought hard to get a proper education and to keep friends of all colors and walks of life.

Together, they endured their father's brutal beatings and verbal assaults. He insisted the girls find the very switches he used to whip them. When their collie, Maime, killed a chicken, he made them watch as he shot the dog with a 12-gauge shotgun.

"Our father, who definitely art not in heaven, at least did one thing right: moving the family to Tampa Bay," Reed said to Debbie when the sisters were grown and independent of the family.

Reed continued to listen to the harmonious, ambient music of Diane Arkenstone.

I can sympathize with Andre, just can't imagine losing sis, she thought, but then pulled herself together, knowing she needed to focus on tonight.

When Ravel called in the new information, she now could complete her plan. All of the pieces were in place. Each team member knew what to do. There wasn't time for rehearsal. All of them would have to play it as it lays.

A card laid is a card played, she reminded herself.

Ravel's call made Reed cautiously optimistic.

Yes, she knew it could all go wrong in several ways.

Indeed, heavy weighs the crown of the leader who puts her people in harm's way.

Reed decided that when all of this was over, she would take a vacation. By herself. And not to Paris, where it was cold and rainy, but somewhere in the Caribbean, where the snorkeling was magnificent, the seafood to die for, and the virgin piña coladas coconut chill.

Aruba, Bonaire, Curacao. The ABC Islands, that's where I'll go, she thought.

Reed finished her cappuccino and readied herself for the night's showdown.

31

———

It was Friday night at Namaste, just past ten-thirty.

Having made it through the lobby metal detector, Raven, Chance, and a young blonde woman strolled into the nightclub. The Doyles were ninety-three minutes late.

Sehar, Tatiana, and the South African Adowa already performed.

The guests had finished their dinners; now they were enjoying coffees and boissons après le dîner.

It was another full house, and the energy was high without being frenetic.

"Look who finally decided to show up," Jake said sarcastically. "Didn't you say Raven promised to arrive at nine p.m.?"

He sat at a VIP front-row table with Reed.

There were three empty chairs at the table.

"Yes, she did say that, and that she was bringing an extra guest."

"Her being so late was on purpose, right, Reed?"

"Absolutely. Raven knows as well as I do that this is it, the big showdown. She simply tried to raise my anxiety level by being oafishly late. She also wants to demonstrate she's in control."

"Didn't work, did it."

Reed *pftted.*

"Not at all. I'm too prepared, too centered, for that little lady to upset me."

Though Jake was unarmed, it helped that Reed had her Glock 9mm holstered under her canary yellow blazer. Her white dress shirt was a Schiffer button down. She wore black jeans with black ankle boots. Reed felt comfortable and safe.

Jake wore the same outfit he had worn all week: beige linen shirt, matching linen pants, brown Mephisto sandals.

Guess it's now sorta my uniform, but I'm retiring it from service once this night is over, he promised himself.

The Doyles approached their table.

Raven seemed tipsy, if not out-and-out drunk.

She and Chance went pure country, sporting denim jackets, white cowboy shirts, blue jeans, and black cowboy boots.

"So, so sorry for being so, so late, my lovelies. Something's come up at the estate, and it's just a challenge. You see, we're playing cat and mouse with a wily critter that just doesn't want to get snared. So we can stay for only an hour."

Hmm, we'll see about that, Reed thought.

She and Jake stood up and shook hands with Raven and Chance.

The young woman hung back.

She wore a black embroidered lace dress with nude stilettos, her blonde locks tied up in a bun.

Raven looked at her.

"Such a pretty girl. Stop hiding, right now. This is a coming-out party for you. Try to think of it as your beaner quinceanera. Sort of, anyway."

Not entirely certain of what Raven just said, the woman nonetheless stepped forward. Tentatively.

"That's my girl. Now, Reed, allow me to introduce you to ...."

Reed offered her hand to the woman.

" ... Sissy, yes, it's a pleasure to finally meet you. I've heard so much about you. And I must say, you are quite photogenic."

Raven was stunned.

How did she know Sissy's name, she wondered.

You're not the only one who does her homework, Reed thought, as she studied the worry lines on Raven's face.

After sizing up each other, Jake and Chance smiled simultaneously.

"How ya been, Jake?"

"Fine, just fine. And you?"

"Can't complain. And I wouldn't anyway. Love that quote from Lou Holtz, let's see now, how does that go?" Chance wondered aloud.

"Holtz said, 'Never tell your problems to anyone. Twenty percent don't care, and the other eighty percent are glad you have them'."

Chance rewarded Jake with his diamond-melting smile.

"My man. Darn shame our women are at odds with one another. I could see myself having a special friendship with you. We could go bow hunting for deer --- I know you're into that. Maybe do some bone fishing in the Keys. Shoot, just a movie night would be cool. We could watch one of my favorite films, *Brokeback Mountain*. What's your favorite line in that movie? Mine is, 'I wish I knew how to quit you.'"

Jake took a moment to digest Chance's proposal.

"That's a great idea, Chance. Movie night would be fine, though I think Reed and Raven should join us. Don't want them to feel excluded. And my favorite line from *Brokeback Mountain*? That's easy: 'This thing, it gets ahold of us again at the wrong place, at the wrong time, and we're dead.' That's fair warning, isn't it?"

"Yes, yes, it is, Jake."

Everyone sat down at the table. Raven sat between Chance and Sissy. She held Sissy's hand.

A server came up to their table.

She had on a white linen long-sleeve blouse and matching slacks complemented by black sandals. Her complexion was porcelain white. The woman's long curly red hair contrasted dramatically with her outfit.

"Good evening, everyone. I'm Athena, and it's my sincere pleasure to be serving you tonight. What can I start you off with?"

Raven broke out in raucous laughter.

"Athena, huh? Woo hoo, that's a good one. So how you doing, Chenoa?"

Chenoa looked at Reed, who simply held her hands up, as if signaling the charade was kaput.

"I'm doing very well, Raven. I trust you are as well."

Raven clapped loudly.

"I knew it, I knew it. Hey next time you go undercover, try wearing a wig. That gorgeous red hair is a dead giveaway."

"Thank you, I'll keep that in mind."

"Goody. Now, as to how I'm doing, I'm fantastic. Especially since I've already had my fair share of the Patron. And I'm just getting warmed up. Time's a wasting! Bring me a margarita, and use that pink Himalayan salt, okey dokey?"

"Of course. And Chance, what would you like to drink?"

He checked out Chenoa before answering.

"I'm driving, Red. Bring me a glass of Hillsborough County tap water. Room temperature. No ice."

Chenoa raised her eyebrows.

"All right, no problem. Sissy, what will you have?"

Sissy looked for guidance from Raven.

"Our little girl will have a Shirley Temple. Listen up, Chenoa, 'cause this is how I want y'all to fix it: muddle two slices of lime and one maraschino cherry; add ice; pour one tablespoon of grenadine syrup, then eight ounces, and no more than eight ounces, of Schweppes ginger ale, and none of that Canada Dry crap. Then shake it like a Polaroid picture, strain it into a martini glass, and garnish it with three maraschino cherries. Got it? If you screw up, I will get thee to a nunnery."

Hmpf, woman thinks she's the ringmaster of my circus, Chenoa thought.

"Yes, ma'am, we'll have the Shirley Temple prepared just as you ordered," Chenoa responded.

People like her make me miss the nunnery a little, she said to herself.

"Reed and Jake, can I freshen your Perrier?"

They nodded yes.

"*Perrier*, can't believe y'all drink that bougie water—stuff's got shark's teeth in it," Raven said.

"Yes, well, Raven, sparkling mineral water is rather an acquired taste," Reed said with a jigger of Southern style sarcasm.

Raven glared at Reed.

"Starting up already? Fine by me. We're only staying here until eleven-thirty, and not a minute longer."

"What's your rush, Raven? We have a special performance planned just for you. Are you afraid your husband's Denali will turn into a pumpkin at midnight?"

If Raven had gotten her margarita, she probably would have thrown it in Reed's face.

"You're poking the mama bear, O'Hara. Not a good idea. I am not impressed with your black belt in tae kwon *don't*. One swipe with these claws of mine would shred that pretty little face of yours."

Reed stayed calm.

Me and my shadow aren't getting along right now, she thought.

"No need to threaten, Raven," Reed said. "I will try to remember your hot-blooded temper. Sorry if I offended you in any way at all. Détente?"

Raven muttered something, then started to relax.

"Yeah, yeah, détente. Where is my darn drink? I'm as thirsty as a Mexicali baking in the Sonoran Desert."

Thankfully, Chenoa arrived with the drink order.

Raven tasted Sissy's Shirley Temple.

"Perfect."

She gave the drink back to Sissy.

"Now let's check out my Margaritaville."

She took a sip.

"That's what I'm talking about. Good job, my Sharona."

Yeah, like I've never heard that before, Chenoa commented sarcastically to herself.

"Chance, darling, how's your water?"

He set down his glass.

"The fluoride bouquet is exquisite, and I'm picking up some phosphate particles with an aftertaste of rusty license plates."

Raven giggled.

"Handsome and brainy. I'm a lucky woman."

Chance tipped his imaginary cowboy hat.

"Couldn't agree with you more, Raven."

Reed sipped from her iced Perrier and set down the tumbler.

"Ready for a performance, Raven?"

She looked quickly at her Guess watch, then said, "Yeah, ready as I'll ever be. Times getting tight, though."

You have no idea how tight your time's getting, Raven Doyle, Reed thought.

She signaled DJ Koala, who wore her signature white silk warm-up track suit with gold piping.

"Mesdames et Messieurs, on stage is Blythe, who has come all the way from London. Let's welcome Blythe with a huge international round of applause."

Everyone clapped wildly.

Blythe stood center stage. She was six-feet tall and thin as a communion wafer. Her long golden hair was in a ponytail. She wore a near-sheer black body suit. Blythe's great passion was jazz dance. Tonight, she would make even the rarely impressed Bob Fosse proud.

DJ Koala put on the Pet Shop Boys' "West End Girls".

The synthpop mashup of a song poignantly captures the vacuous, almost pointless, London life of posh West End young women toying with the wild boys of the East End. Bearing either hearts of glass or hearts of stone, as the song points out, the women and men have no past or future, only the dead-end present.

With its layered bass propelling the song forward, "West End Girls" was an ideal choice for Blythe to showcase jazz dance, a mélange of classical ballet and modern dance. Her knees bent, Blythe kept her body close to the dance floor, using her right foot as a pivot to shift smoothly from one foot to the other. She isolated different parts of her body, incorporating her head, shoulders, arms, rib cage, and hips to make complex, syncopated movements. Her polyrhythms carried two, even three, body rhythms at the same time. Blythe's performance melded the Pet Shop Boys' music with her dance movements, creating a singular, unified artistic performance.

Raven finished her margarita, then motioned for Chenoa to bring another.

"Gotta admit, this English wanker girl is a heckuva dancer, and she's a looker to boot. Too dang tall for my taste though."

"I'm sure Blythe will be crestfallen learning she's not your type," Reed responded.

"Won't let up, will you?" Raven said. "Are you trying to provoke me?"

"No, only having some fun, is all."

Chenoa brought Raven another margarita.

"Raven, I took the liberty of having two shots of Don Julio put in your margarita. Is that okay?"

Raven flopped back in her chair.

"I suppose, but I'm already getting woozy. Heck, I gotta pee, and I don't think I can get up."

She took a large gulp of the double-barreled tequila margarita.

Out came Reed's devilish smile, a grin that suggested she was circling her prey.

"Sissy, you know where the women's restroom is, be a dear and escort Raven there. I think she'll need you to navigate," Reed said.

Sissy was a dear all right, but more like a *deer* lost in the stage lights of Namaste. Knowing she'd be so much Doyle roadkill if she followed Reed's instructions, she instead sat frozen and silent in her chair.

In a snap, Raven spoke up. Loudly.

"A little professional courtesy here, Reed. You don't go around giving commands to another woman's subservient. Only I give orders to Sissy. Besides, my bladder is tight as an iron-clad alibi. I can hold it for as long as I want. No need for me to go near that bathroom."

Not surprised you're afraid to go in that restroom, Reed thought.

"I understand, Raven. My bad for crossing that boundary. Besides, it's best you stay put—our special performance, just for you, is about to begin."

Raven again studied her watch. She again became agitated. She finished her margarita and did not motion to Chenoa for another.

"Whatever, we're leaving in seven minutes, not a second more—even if the dancing ain't done."

Reed casually sipped her Perrier. One dainty sip, then another.

"The performance is a little under nine minutes long. It'll all work out. Trust me, Raven."

Raven lifted her pant leg to above her right boot. She put her hand inside the boot, scratched her leg, leaving the pant leg crumpled atop the boot.

"Trust issues have never been a problem for me. So, let's see this show. I'ma hitting the road real soon."

"Well then, close your eyes," Reed said.

"Huh?"

"Close your eyes and don't open them until the music starts."

"Really, Reed? This is so childish."

"Not childish. Dramatic. Just do it. Please. For me."

Reed put her hand on Raven's hand.

"I'm such a sucker for hot little blondes," Raven said as she closed her eyes.

"Good, now put your hands over your eyes," Reed added.

"For goodness' sake, O'Hara. *Fine.*"

Raven put her hands over her eyes peek-a-boo style, while grumbling, "Feels like I'm back in kindergarten."

DJ Koala stopped the music at the conclusion of John Coltrane's "A Love Supreme."

"Ladies and gentlemen, we're going to make Namaste history tonight. For the first time, there will be *two* performers on stage!"

Stage lights came on.

Raven took her hands away from her eyes to spy Andre and Sierra together on center stage.

In a flash, Benny Goodman's "Sing, Sing, Sing" erupted over the nightclub's sound system.

The ideal song for kicks, flips, and spins, "Sing, Sing, Sing" was recorded in Hollywood on July 6, 1937. It was the quintessential big band song of the swing era. Benny Goodman played on clarinet, Harry James on trumpet, Red Ballard on trombone, and Hymie Schertzer on alto sax. And on drums was Gene Krupa, among the greatest drummers of all time. With Krupa's pulsating tom-tom drum accompaniment, Goodman and his big band created a wide range of thrilling orchestral jazz.

Sierra and Andre began swing dancing right at the start of Krupa's drum opening. Andre wore a black vest and slacks with leather-soled black and white Oxford shoes. Sierra had on a white shirtdress with a black collar, with coordinating black and white Oxfords. Keeping rhythm with the fast-paced "Sing, Sing, Sing", the pair spun and twirled on the dance floor.

Most everyone in the nightclub stood to hoot, holler, and cheer on Andre and Sierra.

Raven stood up as well, though she had a far different take on their performance.

"What in the world is going on," she screamed. "No way that sweaty Black man should be touching that beautiful white woman."

Ignoring Raven, Andre picked up Sierra, swung her on each hip, then pulled her between his legs across the stage.

The feminist in Sierra objected to this classic swing move, but the tactician in her counted on the maneuver to send Raven over the top.

It did.

She threw her double-bowled margarita glass at Andre.

"Quit assaulting her, darkie!"

Andre easily dodged the flying margarita glass, which shattered on the dance floor.

He and Sierra stopped dancing, though DJ Koala kept playing "Sing, Sing, Sing".

Chance got up and stood next to Raven.

"Not cool, Raven, not cool at all. Simmer down and let's get the heck out of here."

Raven slapped Chance in the face.

"I'll decide when we leave."

She swayed slightly.

Once more, she looked at her watch.

"Ah crap! You're right. Time to go, bobo."

Sissy stood up, dutifully waiting to leave with Raven and Chance.

"All of you sit down, our little show isn't over," Reed snarled.

She held her Glock pistol in her right hand, resting it on her lap.

"Reed, I beg of you, we have to *go*" Raven said in slurred anguish.

"You only think you have to go. Trust me, you little twit, you're perfectly safe. All of us are. Now, do sit down. I want you to meet our guests of honor."

Raven and Chance eyed Reed's pistol, while Sissy appeared lost in space.

"Fine, O'Hara, we'll sit down, but only for a couple minutes," Raven said resignedly.

Reed held on to her Glock.

"You'll stay for as long as I tell you to, *Doyle*."

Raven was about to respond when the lights came up in the nightclub.

"Excellent, here come the folks I want you to meet," Reed said.

With Ravel leading the way and Chenoa at the back of the line, Megan, Colt, and Vlad marched toward the VIP table.

Megan wore her uniform from the Hangar.

Colt held an object the size and shape of a Mac Book. He wore his Dallas Cowboys trucker hat.

Vlad had showered and shaved. His outfit most likely came from Chance's wardrobe.

"Oh my word!" Andre exclaimed.

He leapt off the stage and ran to his brother.

The two brothers hugged.

"My baby Vlad, I wasn't sure if I'd get you back, praise to our higher power," Andre cried out. "How did you escape?"

"I first managed to avoid getting whipped, then I hid out in their ridiculous woodshed. It was where the Doyles kept me chained up in the first place."

Andre bit into his fist.

"No, Andre, don't do that. I know what happens when you're done chewing on your hand. It isn't pretty."

Andre lowered his fist.

"But how did you get away from that cracker horse farm?" the older brother asked.

Vlad frowned.

"Do not use cultural slurs around me, my brother. We must rise above such stereotypes."

"You're right. I'm sorry. Sometimes my anger gets the best of me."

"As to how I escaped that evil place, I owe it all to these two."

Vlad nodded toward Colt and Megan.

"Colt was first to discover me in the shed. He could have turned me in, but he didn't. Instead, he helped construct a good hiding spot inside the shed, then enlisted Megan to bring me food, water, and comfort jars, if you know what I mean."

Andre grinned, knowing full well what comfort jars were.

Raven barged into the joyful reunion.

"Well, isn't that such a sweet story? Total bologna, though. I've never seen this darkie in my life."

Colt stepped up to the plate.

"That is a lie! You ordered me and the boys to kidnap Andre. After you realized we'd got the wrong man, you know, not Mr. Andre, you came up with the idea of whipping Vlad. You were gonna use him as a fundraiser by tying him to a cross and selling lashes with a bull whip."

Chance leapt out of his chair.

"What's the matter, Colt? Ticked off Sissy wants me instead of your puny self? I'm going to tear your head off."

Jake got out of his chair.

"No, you're not, Chance. Not on my watch."

With that, he threw a right haymaker at Chance, striking him full in the mouth.

Chance stumbled backwards. He put his hand on his bleeding mouth and found two teeth resting in his palm.

"You, you ... you knocked out my two front teef."

Jake laughed: "Hey, you know what Mike Tyson said, 'Everybody has a plan until they get punched in the mouth.' Besides, now you know what you want for Christmas, you slug."

Jake landed a left uppercut on Chance's chin, then finished him off with a right cross.

Chance collapsed to the floor, down for a ten count.

Raven rushed to her husband.

"My poor baby."

Colt and Megan walked over to Raven.

"We have a little present for you, ma'am. Sissy told me where she hid the bomb in the women's crap ... um ... bathroom on Wednesday night. Megan and I told Ravel, and she passed it onto Miss Reed."

Colt tossed the bomb onto Raven's lap.

"Don't worry, ma'am. Mr. Jake deactivated it long before you showed up tonight."

Raven hissed like a cobra at him.

"Oh, yeah. Almost forgot. I told Miss Reed about Chance killing Jimmie. I also told her where Jimmie's body parts are scattered. Plus, I got the body parts map out of your safe and gave it to Miss Reed. You see, ma'am, Megan and I figured we were next, and we weren't gonna let that happen."

Colt reached out to hold Megan's hand. Megan accepted his gesture.

"You make crossing over real tempting," Megan said. "But we're going to be friends only, okay?"

Colt squeezed her hand delicately.

"For a long time?"

"For a very long time, mate."

Sissy began crying.

"Colt, will you take me back? I promise to be good, like, real good."

"Nope, not gonna happen. Besides, I gotta face up to the evil deeds I was part of. Time for me to man up. Goodbye, Sissy."

Raven scoffed.

"Isn't that just so darling. Makes me want to throw up. Megan, you turned Colt on me, didn't you?"

Megan shook her head no.

"He acted of his own free will, Raven."

"Let me show you some free will, Irish trash."

Raven reached into her right boot and pulled out a ceramic knife. She lunged at Megan, fully intending to stab her in the chest.

"Over here, Raven," Reed said calmly.

Raven looked for only a moment at Reed, who raised her pistol and, from a seated position no less, fired a 9mm round into Raven's right shoulder.

Raven dropped the knife and collapsed next to Chance.

Angry bird *never* gets the worm, Reed thought.

At a table directly behind the VIP table, two men and two women got out of their chairs.

They were not romantically connected to one another; rather, they were plain clothes Sheriff's Deputies, including Homicide Detective Pete Langdon.

Langdon strode over to the Doyles, who were conscious but clearly disoriented.

"Raven and Chance Doyle, you are under arrest on charges of kidnapping, murder, and attempted detonation of an explosive device in a public area."

Langdon then read them their rights.

Chef Glenn brought out a large emergency medical kit and handed it to a deputy.

A Marine corpsman before he became a chef, Glenn offered the deputy some friendly advice as to how best to staunch Raven's wound.

"Looks to me like the round went straight through," Glenn said. "And I've already called in medical. She's going to be fine."

The chef and the deputy fist bumped.

Reed stood by Langdon's side.

"Pete, as usual, you're a saint. Thank you for letting me play this out. No one died tonight and the bad guys are going away for a long time."

"Reed, it has been a true pleasure working with you again. You never fail to bust up my boredom. But listen, I need all of you to stick around and make statements. In a little while, I'll reach out to Tampa PD to smooth their ruffled feathers—I'll make 'em understand why I bird dogged in their neck of the woods."

Reed gave Pete a peck on his right cheek.

"You reach out to me when you're ready to go private."

"Will do—that'd make Rebecca one happy wife."

Jake came up behind Reed, then stood by her side and put his arm around her.

"You okay, my love?" he asked.

Reed exhaled, then leaned her head on Jake's shoulder.

"Yes, I'm all right. Exhausted, stressed, but I'm all right. Talk about a *Seven Days in May* reboot, agree?"

"Absolutely and whenever you're ready, we'll talk about your wounding Raven. We can't let it fester."

"Roger that."

They kissed briefly.

"Reed, let's take off for Paris. Andre and Chenoa can go with us. A long weekend is all I ask."

"Love, all four of us can't be away at the same time."

"Yeah, you're right. So how about this: you mentioned the other night you wanted to fly to Bonaire. All by your lonesome. You need to re-charge. You could kite-surf, fish, snorkel. C'mon, take a week and spread your wings in the Caribbean. We'll keep an eye on things here. No worries."

"Really? You mean that?"

"Yes, of course, and be sure to ride those Paso Finos in Aruba."

Reed hugged Jake.

"You're a good man, Jacob Jordan Dupree."

"You're making me blush, my love."

32

Fourteen-year-old Reed O'Hara had to study a map of the United States in order to locate Clearwater, Florida. A Girl Scout to her core, she sat on the front porch diligently planning the family's journey.

There it is, right in the middle of Florida on the Gulf of Mexico coast, she thought.

She circled on the map her hometown of Charleston, West Virginia, then circled her soon-to-be new hometown of Clearwater.

Using pencil and ruler, she drew a straight line connecting the two cities.

Looks about like nine-hundred miles between them, she thought.

Reed's father had worn out his welcome in Charleston. Constantly shooting off his mouth about white racial superiority, the coup de grâce was his interview with the *Charleston Gazette-Mail*, where he accused gangs of Black students at DuPont Junior High School of harassing his white daughters. Though it was total fabrication on her father's part, Reed ended up being shoved and locked inside her locker by angry Black students.

It was time for the family to leave West Virginia, her father announced.

As he so often did with major decisions, he chose Clearwater, Florida on a whim.

"It's the land of sunshine and oranges," he said. "So let's get packing."

Reed and Debbie did not want to leave Charleston. They had a brigade of friends who were white, Black, and brown. They each had boyfriends. Reed had even let Charley kiss her. Briefly and just once.

Though disappointed about her departure, DuPont Principal Gary Carter tried to cheer her up.

"I've already made a call to the principal at Oak Grove Junior High. I told her all about you. I said she could expect a brilliant and hard-working student to come through her doors."

"Thank you, sir. Still, I'm so sad about not being a Panther."

"Tell you what, I will send you one volume of my Harvard Classics each month. By the time you graduate from ... hmm, let me see ... Clearwater High School, you will have the complete set to take to college."

Reed smiled as her gorgeous blue eyes watered.

"Principal Carter, you are the most generous person I've ever known. I will always remember you, and I promise to stay in contact. You've been like a father to me, and I thank you so much for that."

This time, Principal Carter's eyes watered.

"You're very welcome, young lady. You're about to embark on a great adventure. Make the most of it."

"I will, sir. Goodbye."

Principal and student shook hands.

"Reed, get your butt off that porch and into this car," her father yelled. "Don't make me give you another whipping."

She looked around her neighborhood one last time.

I think I'm ready, she thought.

Reed leapt off the porch and ran to the over-packed family station wagon.

Principal Carter's right, this *will* be a great adventure, and I hope I get to see some pink flamingos, she thought, maybe even some dolphins.

AUTHOR'S NOTES

The following story is as true as a rescued black lab's loyalty to his new master.

The story begins in Tampa Bay in the early seventies. I was in my late teens and living with my family on the Clearwater Beach barrier island anchored in the Gulf of Mexico and only thirty miles from Tampa.

Out of concern for my safety, my parents forbade me from hopping into our lime green '66 Volkswagen Beetle to cross the Courtney Campbell Causeway and partake of Tampa's easy access to alcohol and drugs, strip clubs, and gambling at Derby Lane Greyhound Track and the Tampa Jai Alai Fronton.

To make matters worse, from my parents' standpoint, the Tampa Mafia was in control of most of these alluring vices.

One hot and humid summer evening, my father returned from working in Tampa with a gleevil glint in his icy blue eyes. Standing in the doorway of our home, he resembled Coleridge's ancient mariner about to spin some terrible and forbidding rime.

I wish to be fair to dear old dad. Instead of a dead albatross around his neck, he wore a royal blue silk tie with a perfect Windsor knot, showcased against his white-on-white Jacquard dress shirt.

Earlier that day, my father said with a wisp of a British Isles lilt that he was drinking coffee and finishing up some paperwork in a motel coffee shop on Dale Mabry Highway in South Tampa. He happened to look up as two men in a white Cadillac pulled into the motel's parking lot. They parked in front of a motel room. Not appearing to be in a hurry, the two men climbed out of the orca-sized sedan, opened the car trunk, retrieved two sawed-off shotguns, kicked in the motel room's door, then blasted their way into the room. Seconds later, obviously done with their work, the two men strolled out of the motel room, returned the shotguns to the Caddie's trunk, and leisurely drove away.

My father's only reaction was to ask the waitress to freshen his coffee. Wisely so, he knew better than to be a material witness to this Mafioso hit. Had he stepped forward, he most assuredly would have been found dead in the spacious trunk of his copper Toronado at the Tampa International Airport.

His rime noir was no doubt meant to frighten me away from Tampa. Didn't work, though, as his story made me ache even more to explore Tampa.

See now why I'm enamored with Tampa Bay's bright sun and darkest of dark shade? My home base is a novelist's dream come true. I truly believe I'll never exhaust the motherlode that is Tampa Bay's local color, quirky history, and wonky denizens.

A final and very important point.

Nevermore represents a dramatic shift in my novel writing.

Unlike *Bad Habits* and *Don Coyote*, the first two novels in my Tampa Bay Tropics Thriller series, there's no obscene language, explicit sex, or full-frontal violence in *Nevermore*.

My wife Linda reviewed the first draft of the novel, then urged me to not go so blue. She asked me, instead, to hone my word craft, to push myself artistically, to refrain from posing as a sensationalist and a provocateur.

I listened to Linda, then set about completely rewriting *Nevermore*.

The end result, I believe, may be my best novel.

But not everyone was, or will be, happy I went from Miami Vice to Nick at Night Nice.

My friend and fellow writer Randy "Doc" Sexton was disappointed I moved away from the unblinking violence and steamy sex spiced with salty dog verbiage so prevalent in my debut novel, *Bad Habits*.

I'm not surprised by Doc's disappointment. There's nothing pink tea about this worldly man. After all, I met Doc in a centuries-old salsa hall on a rainy Saturday night deep in the Barrio Viejo of Cartagena, Columbia. I neither confirm nor deny that Doc sat next to his femme fatale Jackie with two shot glasses and a near-empty bottle of Patron between them, and a Browning 9mm semi-automatic resting on the table near Doc's right hand. Well, that's how I remember it.

Sorry, Doc, you are going to have to get used to the new me.

In closing, writing *Nevermore* was transformative for me, since I now strive to maintain a healthy gestalt in my life. As Linda taught me, I feed the good wolf and starve the bad wolf both personally and professionally.

Thank you, Linda, for such life-changing advice. No man could desire more from a woman as remarkable and inimitable as yourself. I love you dearly.

Until we cross paths again, folks, be well and keep an open mind.

Bread and Roses,
George L. Fleming
AuthorGeorgeFleming@gmail.com

ABOUT THE AUTHOR

George Fleming is a former journalist and college writing instructor. He earned a bachelor's degree in English from Florida State University and a master's degree in English from Purdue University.

Fleming graduated from Clearwater High School, where he first met Linda. It was not until college that Linda gave in to his overtures. Married on August 18, 1979, George and Linda set out in a '70 VW Beetle to begin a life filled with adventures, mishaps, sorrows, and great wonders.

George and Linda have two adult daughters, Margo and Jennifer, and three granddaughters, Cloe, Mya and Macy, most of whom continue to live in Tampa Bay.

Fleming also is the author of BAD HABITS and DON COYOTE, the first and second novels of the TAMPA BAY TROPICS THRILLER series. Hard at work on BONAIRE BLONDE, the fourth installment in the series, Fleming remains on track to write twenty novels in twenty years.

COMING SOON

BONAIRE BLONDE

A Tampa Bay Tropics Thriller

By George L. Fleming

AuthorGeorgeFleming@gmail.com